Behind her, she heard the pounding of horses' hooves and turned to see if a neighbor was coming to visit.

She lifted her hand over her eyes and scanned the riders. Her heart nearly plunged to her feet. She sucked in a gasp. *No, it couldn't be.*

Katie lifted her skirts, turned back toward the farm, and ran for all she was worth. *Father, help me!*

The horses quickly closed the space, and Katie found herself surrounded by a pack of unkempt men whose expressions reminded her of ravenous wolves. The horses snorted and stamped their hooves. Katie stopped to catch her breath while her mind raced for a way to escape.

"Well, well, who would have thought you'd make things so easy?"

Katie cringed at the grating voice she had never expected to hear again.

VICKIE MCDONOUGH is an award-winning author who believes God is the ultimate designer of romance. She is a wife of thirty-one years, mother to four sons, and a doting grandma. When not writing, she enjoys reading, watching movies, and traveling. Visit Vickie's Web site at www.vickiemcdonough.com.

Books by Vickie McDonough

HEARTSONG PRESENTS
HP671—Sooner or Later
HP716—Spinning Out of Control

The Bounty Hunter
and the Bride

Vickie McDonough

Heartsong Presents

This book is dedicated to my parents, Harold and Margie Robinson. Mom and Dad never failed to allow me to stretch my adventurous wings, even when that meant buying a horse, though we lived in the city, or buying a motorcycle when I was only fourteen. I think the freedom they allowed me as a child gave me the boldness I needed to begin writing and pursue publishing. Dad is now playing his trumpet in heaven and keeping the angels laughing, and Mom is encouraging me with her faithful prayers.

A note from the Author:
I love to hear from my readers! You may correspond with me by writing:

Vickie McDonough
Author Relations
PO Box 721
Uhrichsville, OH 44683

ISBN 978-1-59789-388-6

THE BOUNTY HUNTER AND THE BRIDE

All scripture quotations are taken from the King James Version of the Bible.

All of the characters and events in this book are fictitious. Any resemblance to actual persons, living or dead, or to actual events is purely coincidental.

Our mission is to publish and distribute inspirational products offering exceptional value and biblical encouragement to the masses.

PRINTED IN THE U.S.A.

one

"You oughta be right proud of yourself."

City Marshal Dusty McIntyre's chest swelled at Deputy Tom Barker's comment. Then he heaved a sigh of relief, knowing the crafty swindler he'd been after for months was finally behind bars. He eyed the solemn prisoner in the cell. "I have to admit, there were days I wondered if we'd ever catch this weasel. Feels good to have him locked up."

Ed Sloane's eyes narrowed as he glared through the bars. "Just 'cause you got me locked up today, Marshal, don't mean you will tomorrow." One cheek kicked upward in a cocky sneer.

Dusty wanted to smack that belligerent look off Sloane's face, but he wouldn't. As a law officer, he was bound by a different code than the man in his jail, and as a Christian, he was called by God to walk a straight path and control his temper. He recognized Ed Sloane for what he was—a lost man. A man on the road to hell if he didn't change his ways real fast.

Sloane stuck his hands between two bars. "Think you could take these cuffs off now that you got me safe in your jail?"

Dusty didn't miss the sarcasm that laced his prisoner's voice. The man still didn't seem to realize he'd been caught. Much as he'd like to leave Sloane handcuffed, he crossed the room, his boots echoing on the wood floor. He pulled a warm metal key from his shirt pocket, but then stopped and glanced at Tom. "If he tries anything, shoot him."

Tom pressed his lips together and nodded as he pulled his pistol from his holster and pointed it in Sloane's direction. "Be happy to."

Dusty approached the cell with caution. Ed Sloane was slipperier than a greased hog at the county fair. A chill slipped up Dusty's spine when an evil glint flashed in the man's light blue eyes. What could bring a man to be so depraved that he would prey on the elderly and widows, stealing them blind and leaving them penniless and heartbroken?

With a few rattles and clicks, the handcuffs were off, and Dusty moved back. Sloane gave a guttural laugh that sounded like a snarling, wounded animal. Shaking his head, Dusty crossed the room to his desk and tossed down the key. Tom picked it up, stuck it in the desk drawer, and then holstered his weapon.

"Don't you reckon you oughta head home to supper and tell that fine wife of yours all about your exceptional day?" Tom grinned, and his thick mustache twitched. "If she's fixin' that rhubarb pie of hers, you might save me a slice—if you've a mind to. Mmm-mm, it's mighty fine."

"I may do just that." Dusty smiled at his deputy. Tom had been his best friend since school days, and it seemed natural to hire him as his deputy when Dusty's father retired as city marshal of Sanders Creek, in the Oklahoma territory, and Dusty took over. Most of the time he worked days and Tom evenings, but lately they'd both been pulling almost twenty-four-hour shifts as their search for Sloane narrowed. They'd gone from house to house, ranch to ranch, searching for Sloane and his gang. His trail resembled that of a cyclone, leaving in its wake a path of desperation and destruction. Now that Dusty had captured Sloane, it shouldn't be too hard to get the rest of his gang.

Dusty's belly grumbled, and he yawned. All he wanted was to eat one of Emily's fine meals, then hit the hay and sleep a full day and night.

Except for Sloane and the havoc he and his gang had caused lately, this past year had been the best Dusty could remember. First, he'd given his heart to God. Then five months ago, he'd fallen in love and married the new banker's daughter.

He longed to run his fingers through Emily's thick, auburn hair. Soft as a horse's muzzle, but as sweet smelling as the rose-bushes in front of their porch. He imagined her pine green eyes twinkling with merriment as she played one of her little pranks on him. An only child, Dusty couldn't wait until they had a house full of children. Emily would be a wonderful mother, and he could only hope he'd be a decent father. God would help him in that area.

Ah yes, life was good.

A cowboy on a bay horse rode past at a quick trot, slinging dust on him and yanking him from his thoughts. Frantic shouts at the end of the street chased away his warm feelings, and a snake of apprehension slithered down his spine. Looking around, he noticed men running and women with skirts lifted high hurrying around the corner up ahead. He picked up his pace and jogged to the end of Main Street, then turned onto Haskell Avenue. Two blocks down, he saw the source of everyone's anxiety. His heart thudded to a stop just as his feet did.

One of his neighbors' houses was engulfed in flames, but the billowing smoke was so thick that he couldn't determine which one it was. He narrowed his eyes and studied the scene. Men ran everywhere, using anything from hats to mixing bowls to dip in the nearby horse troughs and get water to throw onto the fire.

Dusty charged forward, fearing for his friends. Was it old man Harper and his sickly wife's home? Or maybe the two-story clapboard building that housed a pair of widowed sisters who had recently been victims of Ed Sloane? They sure didn't need any more trouble.

Dusty's legs propelled him closer. As the roof collapsed on the only blue house in the area, he felt as if he'd been speared by an Indian's lance. Realization dawned like a heavy, dark curtain being lifted on a stage of performers. Only this was no theatrical show. This was his life. His home.

Dusty raced forward, screaming for his wife. "E—Emily! Emily!"

Heads turned his way, and shoulders drooped. Dusty didn't want to read the expressions in those faces covered with black soot. Strong arms pulled him back just as he reached his porch. His face stung from the heat of the flames, and he fought his captors but wasn't strong enough to outmaneuver four big men.

He turned away from the scene, feeling the heat bleed through his shirt onto his back. Across the street from the flaming remains of his house, a group of women stood, each one holding her hand or a handkerchief over her nose.

Sympathetic eyes stared back.

No! This couldn't be happening. Everything he owned was in that house. Dusty backed out of his friends' hold and ran to Harmon Styles, a neighbor who lived around the corner. "Have you seen Emily? I need to make sure she's okay."

Harmon's concerned gaze darted toward the man standing next to him. Pastor Phillips reached out his hand to Dusty's shoulder. "I'm sorry, son. We tried hard to save her."

A fog enveloped Dusty's head, making it hard to see and comprehend. "What? Just tell me where she is." He looked right, then left. Nowhere did he see his beloved's face.

"E—Emily!" Choking on the swirling smoke, he dropped to his knees. Where was she? His tired mind struggled to remember if this was the day she'd gone to her sewing circle. No, that was Tuesday. This was Wednesday.

God, no. Please find my wife. Let her be safe. I need her.

Pastor Phillips stooped down beside him, offering a cup of water. Dusty shook his head. He didn't want water. He had to locate Emily. As he started to rise, he caught the minister's pained expression. "I'm so sorry, son, but she's gone. Thelma Sue—she saw Emily in the side windows hurrying toward the front door just before the roof collapsed. We tried to save her. We truly did. It just happened too fast."

Dusty ducked his head, unable to grasp the pastor's words. His legs trembled like never before, forcing him to press his hands against the ground to keep from collapsing. *God, don't do this to me. Emily is my life.*

The top of his head touched the ground as tears blurred his vision and grief pierced his heart. Friends gathered near, patting his shoulder and offering whispers of sympathy.

Dusty lifted his head, peering through several pairs of legs to see the burning mass that had been his home. The flaming remains of the roof rested at an odd angle, like a sinking ship. As he watched, the bricks of the chimney he'd repaired only a month ago crashed down, sending more smoke and fiery embers into the air.

Anger surged through his being as he realized all his dreams had just gone up in smoke. He growled and shoved upward like a wounded bear, sending his friends scattering from the force.

His eyes burned as his hopes and dreams were reduced to ashes. He had to get away from this crowd.

Pressing his hat down low on his forehead, he turned away from the scene. Why hadn't Emily answered his call? *No!* She couldn't be gone. His mind couldn't comprehend the emptiness of life without her. Just this morning, she'd kissed him good-bye and promised to have her delicious fried chicken waiting for him.

He pressed the heel of his hand against his forehead, trying to make sense of it all. *Oh, Emily.*

Somewhere behind him, he heard running footsteps and someone screaming. "No! Please. Emily Sue!"

He recognized his mother-in-law's frantic pleading but had no power to comfort her. The woman's screams tore at his battered heart. How could God let this happen? "Marshal! Where's the marshal?"

A voice from far away pulled him out of the darkness sucking him under. Hank Slaughter, owner of the mercantile across from the jail, plowed through the crowd of gawkers and hurried toward him. "There's been a jailbreak, Marshal. Tom's been shot."

Shoving down his hat, Dusty moved forward as if living a nightmare. His mind refused to believe Emily had perished. She was simply at a friend's house. He had no trouble slipping into work mode. It was just what he needed to drive the frightful thoughts from his mind.

His boots pounded out a cadence on the boardwalk as he jogged toward his office. *Emily is gone. Emily is gone.* Even the wood under his feet screamed the words.

No! He wouldn't believe it. He couldn't. Any minute now he would wake up and find out this was just a nightmare.

He hurried inside the jailhouse, blinking as his eyes adjusted to the dim lighting. The faint odor of gunpowder clung to the air, and the empty jail cell with the door swung open mocked him. Doc Michaels knelt on the floor beside Tom, examining his bloody shoulder wound. He looked up as Dusty skidded to a halt. "He'll live."

Relief coursed through him like a flash flood. Squatting, he stared into Tom's pain-filled eyes. "What happened?"

"Three men." Tom's eyes closed, his mouth contorted as he fought for control. "Got the best of me. Sloane escaped." He heaved a deep breath. "Headed north."

Dusty turned around to start recruiting a posse but then decided he needed to do this alone. Reaching down, he squeezed Tom's good shoulder. "Don't worry about it, pardner. I'll get him back. You just get better."

He started to turn, but Tom grabbed his pant leg. "Wait—"

The glazed look of despair in his friend's eyes nailed him in place.

"Your house. It's okay?"

Dusty crinkled his brow. Tom had no way of knowing what

had happened. He stooped to get closer, pushing back an ominous premonition. "Why?"

"As Sloane left, he looked back—said he'd left a present at your house."

Dusty stood and backed up until he hit the wall. A muscle in his jaw twitched.

Sloane couldn't be responsible for the fire, could he? Had the fire simply been a diversion to allow Sloane's escape?

"Glad things are all right. . . ." Tom lost consciousness as Doc Michaels wrapped his shoulder.

"You men, carry the deputy over to my office," the doctor said.

As several men shuffled around him, Dusty mentally listed what supplies he needed. Two rifles and ammunition. Some food. His canteen and horse. He unlocked the rifle case, grabbed two Winchesters, and then locked it back up again. On his way out the door, he yanked his brown duster off a hook and studied the crowd. He couldn't stand seeing the sympathetic looks from the townsfolk. His gaze landed on Steve Foster, a local businessman who had once been a deputy. "You'll watch over things till I get back or Tom's on his feet again?"

Steve pressed his lips together and nodded.

Dusty strode back into his office, yanked open the middle drawer of his desk, and grabbed a deputy's badge. He flipped it to Steve as he tramped outside. As he moved off the boardwalk, the crowd in the street parted like the Red Sea. Dusty turned toward the livery, pulling his hat down low on his forehead so he wouldn't have to meet anyone's gaze.

Tears blurred his vision. Emily was gone. . .and Sloane

was to blame. For now, he'd focus on capturing Sloane and seeing him hanged or in prison for life. Later he'd think of his beautiful wife and all that he'd lost.

⅋

Dusty followed Sloane's trail until dark. He dismounted and tried to grab a few hours' sleep, but every time he closed his eyes, he saw flames and imagined Emily screaming for him. If only he hadn't dawdled at the jail, gloating over Sloane's capture. Maybe he could have stopped the fire before it had gotten out of control. Maybe he could have gotten Emily out of the house before it was too late.

By sunup, he'd eaten a dried-out biscuit and an apple and was on the trail again. Thankfully, last night about dusk, he'd happened upon the unusual, square-shaped hoofprints he recognized as belonging to Sloane's horse. After weeks of trailing Sloane before, Dusty would never forget that unique track.

As the sun reached its zenith, Dusty stared out over a valley that led into Kansas. He had no jurisdiction there. Truth be told, he hadn't had any legal authority to chase Sloane since he left Garfield County. His horse snorted, impatient to move on.

A red-tailed hawk glided across the sky, then dove toward the ground and soared upward again with a squirming rabbit in its grip. Dusty felt like that hare.

His life was over. His home gone. His wife dead. And his God had abandoned him.

Dusty glanced down, and a ray of sunlight flashed off his marshal's badge. Yanking off the metal star, he rubbed his thumb over its smooth surface. He'd dedicated his life to protecting the townsfolk of Sanders Creek in the Oklahoma

Territory, but he'd failed to protect the person he loved most. Clenching his jaw, he flipped the badge in the air and watched the sun reflect off it as the silver star spiraled to the ground.

With his heels, he nudged his horse forward. If it was the last thing he did, he'd find Ed Sloane and see justice done.

two

Katie Hoffman jumped at the fervent pounding on her bedroom door. "Yes?"

"Uhh. . .Miz Hoffman, the judge is here, and that feller you're fixin' to marry is gettin' fidgety."

Katie smiled at her shy ranch hand's muffled comment, knowing he must be embarrassed to his boot tips to be talking through her bedroom door. "Thank you, Carter. Tell them I'm almost ready and will be out in a moment." She could imagine Allan King, her fiancé, pacing the parlor, checking his pocket watch over and over, and driving everyone loco. He'd been after her to marry him for two months now, and he wasn't one to be patient.

She turned and studied her reflection in the tall mirror. "Katie King. Mrs. Allan King. Has a pretty nice ring to it, if I do say so myself." She fastened the final button of the blue-gray cotton dress, which draped over her protruding stomach and fell in soft waves to the ground. The ecru Irish-lace collar looked pretty against her tanned neckline. Her spirits soared to be wearing something colorful again instead of widow's black.

She touched her cheek. Did Allan mind that her skin wasn't fair, as was popular with the women in town? Jarrod had said he loved her coloring, but then, even her tanned skin had looked pale against her first husband's bronze complexion. Growing up a tomboy, she'd been outside so often that her skin was always a golden brown and her hair a light blond. After she married, she'd tried harder to stay inside or always wear a bonnet, but since Jarrod's death, the farm demanded so much more of her that she now spent much of her day outside. With the brisk winds that often swept across the Oklahoma plains, she found it easier to work without a hat, which frequently blew off anyway; thus her hair had again lightened and her skin darkened.

Katie pushed in another hairpin to secure her thick bun, then eased down onto the chair beside the window to put on her shoes. As her palm came to rest on her large belly, the child within heaved a mighty kick, making her hand bounce. Not for the first time, she wondered if Jarrod had given her a son or daughter.

Leaning her head against the tall back of the rocker, she studied the bedroom that she had shared with Jarrod. White eyelet curtains fluttered as a cool breeze tickled their hem. The Wedding Ring quilt she'd labored over most of one winter was pieced together from blue and white scraps of fabric and now covered the bed she would soon share with her new husband. It had been Jarrod's suggestion to paint the room a pale blue, and she had to admit she liked it. But would Allan? He seemed a tad particular about things.

Tears stung her eyes, but she batted them away. This wasn't the time for crying. Those days were past. She was getting married for the second time in less than a year and should consider herself fortunate to have found a man willing to wed a woman in her condition.

She thought back to the day she'd met Allan. He'd shown

up on her doorstep with a cheery smile on his handsome face and holding a newspaper carrying the ad she'd placed for the sale of her farm. Selling would allow her to pay off the mortgage and give her funds to live off until the baby arrived and she could find some type of work to do.

Before purchasing the farm, Allan had insisted on examining every aspect of the property and equipment. As they'd spent hours together going through the barn, touring the land, and reviewing the books, Katie had grown accustomed to his presence. One afternoon, he'd taken her to nearby Claremont for dinner at the new hotel. She smiled at the memory of the fancy dining room and delicious food. Her mouth watered just thinking about the fresh trout, the abundant vegetables, and the creamy ice cream she'd eaten that night. Maybe he'd take her there again sometime.

Allan's charming personality and constant pampering were a balm to her lonely, grieving spirit. Soon, instead of talking about buying the farm, he was begging her to marry him. And she'd finally given in. It hadn't taken too long for her to see that marrying him was the only way to save her baby's inheritance. By marrying Allan, she could keep the farm and have him, too.

Katie sighed. She would have preferred to grieve over Jarrod longer, but Allan had swooped in and taken her by surprise. In this day and time, a woman did what she had to do to get by. It was very common for women, especially those with children, to remarry quickly, foregoing the customary mourning period. Surely God had sent Allan to her. Katie shook her head. Enough of this debating. She'd made her choice.

Standing, she crossed the room and stared out the window at her large farm. She and Jarrod had made such great plans for this place. What would he think about her marrying again so soon after the accident that had taken his life? Would he understand the farm was simply too much for her to handle without him, especially with a baby on the way?

Crossing the room to the oak chest of drawers, she picked up a photograph taken on her first wedding day. She'd been so hopeful and naive, with no premonition of the disaster soon to come. She studied Jarrod's sturdy face, then placed a kiss against the cool glass covering the picture. Who could have imagined things would turn out like they had? Jarrod died never even knowing he was going to be a father. "You'd have been a wonderful dad. I'll never forget the love and laughter we shared, sweetheart. Good-bye, my love. See you in heaven someday."

Katie opened the top drawer and slid the picture under her unmentionables. Her fingers lingered on the smooth gold of her wedding band. After a final moment of hesitation, she slid it off and placed it on Jarrod's picture.

She smoothed her hand across her stomach. She might not love Allan as she had Jarrod, but he would be good to her, her child would have a father, and she would no longer have to struggle running the farm alone.

She slipped on a pair of cream-colored gloves to hide her rough hands and chipped fingernails, and inhaling a strengthening breath, she lifted her head and opened the bedroom door. It was time to get married.

Her footsteps echoed down the narrow, dimly lit hallway to the parlor. The smells of old wood and furniture polish battled with the fragrant scent of chicken baking in the oven. Being so much with child, she had decided to get married at home rather than at the church in town, and afterward, they all would enjoy a good meal before the judge departed.

As she glided into the parlor, all heads turned in her direction. Allan looked striking in his new three-piece gray suit, and she was sure that was a glint of victory she'd seen flash in his icy blue eyes. They reminded her of a cold winter's morning when the fog still clung to the earth. He had a right to look satisfied; he'd finally gotten her to consent to marry him.

The smile she gave him turned to a frown when she noticed Judge Simons sitting on the sofa, nursing a glass of whiskey. Allan moved his hand, and the lamplight reflected off the empty glass he also held. Disappointment coursed through her. She lifted an eyebrow at him. He knew she objected to having liquor in the house, so why was it here?

His expression remained cool, and he shrugged. "Surely you can't object to a man toasting his own wedding." He slapped the glass down with a clink on the fireplace mantle as if daring her to oppose him.

She certainly could object but didn't want to start an argument before she was even married. Turning away, her gaze fell on the Hoffman family Bible. In that instant, she realized she'd never asked Allan if he believed in God. Since he'd been so kind and helpful, she'd assumed he was a Christian. Surely, he must be. He'd gone to church with her nearly every Sunday since they'd met. She shook off a shiver of concern.

The rotund Judge Simons smacked his empty glass on the end table next to the settee. "Shall we begin?"

He looked over the top of his spectacles at her, and a flash of regret pierced her heart for not having a minister marry them. Using the arm of the settee for support, the judge heaved his large body upward and ambled toward the fireplace.

As she crossed the room to stand beside Allan, she smiled

at Carter and Sam, her two ranch hands. They were the only guests in attendance. Another stab of guilt sliced at her for not letting Uncle Mason and Aunt Rebekah know she was getting married again. She wasn't up to all the hoopla and family members they would have brought with them. Uncle Mason would have drilled Allan on his family history and his spiritual well-being. Aunt Rebekah would never have let her have such a simple wedding. And she'd been too embarrassed to admit to her neighbors that she was marrying so soon after Jarrod's death—not that six months was all that soon. She couldn't help wondering what her friends would say when they found out she had married Allan King.

The judge cleared his throat, and Katie cast aside her reservations and feelings of guilt. She was doing what she had to do to keep her farm and to provide her child with a father.

"Dearly beloved." The judge's huge cheeks puffed up even bigger than normal as a belch escaped.

Katie closed her eyes, blinking back stinging tears. This wedding so paled in comparison with her first one. She didn't even have a flower bouquet or anyone to give her away.

She looked into Allan's eyes to draw support but was met with his smoldering gaze. His slicked-back black hair glistened like a raven's wing, and his full lips twitched, reminding her of the times he'd stolen kisses. She shivered, wondering if she could be the wife he'd surely want. She moistened her dry lips with the tip of her tongue, and his mouth pulled sideways in a one-sided grin.

Her heart pounded a frenzied beat. This was what she wanted, wasn't it? To be Mrs. Allan King?

Turning back to Judge Simons, she realized she hadn't heard a word he'd said.

"If there be anyone here who objects to this union, speak now or forever hold your peace." The judge lowered his spectacles, his bushy eyebrows pulled together into a single line, and he glared at Carter and Sam. The two ranch hands looked at each other, then shrugged. Katie knew Carter didn't approve of Allan, probably because he was still loyal to Jarrod; but Sam was a new employee, and Katie had no clue why he, too, seemed uncomfortable in Allan's presence. Still, she had faith Allan would soon win both men over as he had her.

When nobody responded, the judge continued. "Do you, Edward Allan King, take Katherine Ann Hoffman to be your wedded wife?"

"You bet. She kept me waiting long enough." Allan smiled down at her, his eyes filled with something that made her swallow hard. Her quivering legs barely held her up. He squeezed her hand and turned back toward the judge. Funny, he'd never told her Allan was his middle name.

The judge looked over his glasses at her. "Do you, Katherine Ann Hoffman, take Edward Al—"

The front door burst open and slammed against the wall, rattling the windowpanes. Katie jumped and pivoted around. Cool October air charged in, followed by a cowboy with a gleaming silver pistol in his hand. Dressed mostly in black except for a stained brown duster, he stood surveying the room, his eyes barely showing under the black hat pulled low onto his forehead. Allan grabbed her upper arms and pulled her in front of him as if she were a shield. His quickened breath warmed her nape even as chills of fear raced down her spine. *Who is this stranger? What does he want?*

Footsteps echoed on the front porch, and Marshal Dodge from Claremont strode in. "I told you to wait for me, McIntyre."

His gaze flew past Katie and landed on Allan. "That him?"

The cowboy's lips thinned to a straight white line, and a muscle in his jaw twitched. He shoved his hat back on his forehead. Coal black eyes glared at Allan, and he nodded. "We meet again, Sloane."

Allan's fingertips dug into Katie's arms. Her heart pounded like a blacksmith's hammer. *Who is Sloane? Why is the marshal here?*

She glanced at Carter and Sam, who'd backed up against the wall, eyes wide in confusion. Too bad they weren't wearing their holsters. If only she hadn't requested they not wear them during the wedding. But then if the marshal was there, surely they were safe from this stranger.

The judge slithered away, leaving only Allan and Katie in the gunman's path.

The marshal reached for his gun, and Allan muttered a curse that made Katie cringe. Suddenly, he shoved her forward. Her heart jolted; confusion circled her mind. She took two quick steps, then stumbled on the hem of her long dress, falling forward. Fear clutched her being, and her only thoughts were to protect her child. Katie reached for the side of the settee but missed. Her shoulder collided with the settee's wood trim as she fell under the round-topped end table. She reached out to break her fall, but a stinging sensation shot through her hand and wrist, stampeding up her arm. She landed hard, the table's wooden feet biting into her side. Pain surged like a flash flood throughout her body.

"Get 'im!" the cowboy yelled as he charged toward Allan. A ruckus erupted in the room. Men flew in different directions.

Katie sucked in several slow breaths, trying to maintain control and keep from fainting. Had Allan actually shoved her? The ache in her heart matched the one in her wrist.

With her good hand, she pushed herself onto her back. She lifted her injured arm and laid it across her chest. Wincing, she watched the judge slink out the front door like a fat snake with Sam close on his heels. Marshal Dodge fanned out to the left, the cowboy inched forward toward Allan in the middle, and Carter moved to the cowboy's right side.

Squinting through her pain, Katie saw Allan's gaze, steady and measured, as if trying to figure out how to take on three men. She wanted to yell that this was a mistake. They had the wrong house. The wrong man. But she couldn't find the strength to force the words out.

"So, McIntyre, how's your deputy? He still alive?" Allan hiked his chin and hissed the words in the cowboy's direction. His eyes glinted. "And how's that pretty little wife of yours?"

The stranger stiffened, then yelled and charged Allan. Moving at the same time, Allan rushed toward her. Katie's heart soared. Was he coming to help her?

The next instant, he leaped onto the gold brocade chair that sat beside the end table, stepped up onto the back, and then dove through the window above her head. Glass shattered and rained shards on top of her like a hailstorm. The chair spun around on one leg, then toppled back, landing with a dull thud and sharp stab on her left ankle. She squealed from the intense pain.

The cowboy lunged out the window right behind Allan. Marshal Dodge and Carter charged out the front door. The marshal shoved Carter out of his way, knocking him against the hall tree that sat next to the door. Carter regained his balance and hurried outside, leaving her alone.

The hall tree teetered back and forth, then tumbled away

from her, landing with a crash on a small round table. Katie held her breath as the beautiful hurricane lamp Jarrod had given her as a wedding gift toppled to the floor and shattered. A sharp stab of loss lanced her heart. Flames ignited, licking at a zigzag trail of oil across her carpet. The breeze blowing through the door fed the blaze that grew in frantic intensity. Katie's eyes widened, and she covered her stomach as she realized the danger she was in.

"Dear Lord, please help me!" she cried, fighting her overwhelming fear as the room filled with smoke and she watched the home she and Jarrod had built being destroyed.

She had to get out of the house! Was nobody was coming to rescue her? Where had all the men gone? She wanted to cry over Allan's desertion, but she had to stay focused.

"Stay calm. Don't panic." She took a steadying breath, ignored the shooting pain in her hand, and tried to get up. Pressed against the wall with the heavy chair across her legs, she couldn't move her cumbersome body. Her heart pounded. Her breath came in staccato gasps.

Flames fanned out in all directions like a furious lynch mob seeking its victim. Her long lace curtains *poofed* ablaze, and she watched as the fire raced upward. Fighting her fear, she struggled and squirmed with all her might. One foot broke free, but the chair still held her dress and other leg prisoner. She'd always hated that chair. Why hadn't she gotten rid of it before now?

Hampered by her long skirt, in desperation, she shoved with her foot, trying again and again to move the heavy chair. Each kick only made the chair bite into her leg more. *This can't be happening.*

Tears burned her eyes as thick smoke scorched her throat.

She coughed and covered her face with her sleeve. Would this be her last day on earth? Would she die without seeing her baby's face? Without her child taking its first breath of life?

No! She wouldn't give up without a fight. She writhed and wrestled the chair that held her captive. The child inside her tumbled around as if joining in the effort to get free.

"Help me, Lord. Somebody help me!"

three

Dusty tucked in his chin and closed his eyes as he dove out the window right behind Sloane. His hard landing jolted his shoulder and hip. He rolled off the edge of the porch and onto his feet. Sloane was only ten paces ahead, dashing toward the marshal's horse. Dusty burst into a run, hoping his long legs would give him an advantage.

Just as Sloane slowed to mount the bay mare, Dusty lunged through the air and hit him behind the knees. Sloane smacked hard against the horse and bounced off, tumbling backward over Dusty and onto the ground. The mare squealed and pranced sideways. Dusty struggled to his feet and flung himself across Ed Sloane's body.

Weak with relief at finally catching his man, Dusty pressed himself across Sloane's back as the man bucked and struggled to get free. Dusty heard footsteps, then the rattle of handcuffs as the marshal secured Sloane's hands—then Sloane's curse.

"Got him." Heaving from exertion, the marshal waved Dusty off.

Dusty sat back on his heels, breathing hard and staring at the lowly scoundrel who had ruined his life. He wanted to pummel Sloane's face and watch him beg for mercy, but he wouldn't yield to that temptation.

Although dirt and dried grass clung to Sloane's disheveled hair and clothing, he smirked. "I got away once. I can do it again."

Dusty clenched his fist and ground his teeth together as the memory of that awful day resurfaced—the day his wife had died and Sloane had escaped. He stood and took a step toward his nemesis, but then turned away with his fists at his sides, staring out across the acres of barren farmland. Slugging Sloane wouldn't bring Emily back or ease his pain.

"You ain't gettin' out of my jail."

Dusty turned around at the sound of the marshal's voice, grateful for the man's help in capturing Sloane.

The lawman hauled Sloane to his feet. "You there—" He pointed to the other man who'd helped chase Sloane, one who had been at the wedding. "Help me get this crook on that gelding."

Dusty watched as the two men lifted Sloane onto the spare horse the marshal had brought with them. A wave of relief and satisfaction washed over him at finally capturing his man. Dusty sucked in a breath and nearly gagged on a whiff of smoke. Spinning around, heart pounding, he faced his nightmare again.

Flames raced up the curtains inside the two-story farmhouse, sending a cloud of smoke barreling out the broken window and open door. The memory of another house burning singed his thoughts.

A woman's scream rent the cool afternoon. Dusty surged into motion, realizing Sloane's bride was still inside. He wouldn't let another woman die—not if he had the power to save her.

The marshal turned to assist him, but Dusty waved him off. "Stay with Sloane."

Running toward the house, he pulled his bandanna over his mouth and nose and jerked off his duster. He leaped up the steps and stopped just inside the front door. Angry flames had branched out from what looked like the remains of an oil lamp. Thick smoke clung to the ceiling and drifted downward.

Where was the woman? He dropped to his knees and crawled inside, his gaze darting one way and then another, eyes stinging from the thick smoke. Where had he last seen her?

By the broken window! He had reached out to try to break her fall when Sloane had cast her aside, but she'd been too far away. Pivoting to his left, he noticed a chair had tumbled across the lady's skirt. He crawled forward, ignoring the sharp stings in his hands as they landed on shards of glass.

Dusty tossed the chair to the side. Frantic blue eyes softened with relief. The woman coughed and tried to rise, but he could tell that she was in terrible pain. He swooped down and picked her up, even as she struggled.

"I—I can walk."

With her in his arms, he hurried toward the front door. Behind him, a wall crashed down, sending billows of smoke around them. The woman's harsh cough blasted his ear again and again.

Dusty didn't want to think how close he'd come to causing another woman's death. At least this one should survive. He could only hope the fall and the smoke wouldn't somehow affect the child she carried.

When they neared the barn, Dusty set her on the back of a buckboard. Tears streamed down her face, making rivulets in the soot on her cheeks. She gazed past him at her home. A look of total loss on her face made his heart clench.

This was his fault. If he'd waited a few more minutes for the marshal instead of plunging ahead on his own, they might have captured Sloane without this woman losing her home or getting hurt.

As he considered the scene inside the house when he had barged in, he realized a wedding had been in progress. He narrowed his eyes and studied the woman again, not allowing her tears to affect him. Why in the world would she be marrying Ed Sloane? Could the child she bore possibly belong to him?

⁊⊷

Katie couldn't stop the tears blurring her vision. She laid her throbbing wrist across her stomach, cradled it with her other arm, and stared at her home. Like an angry monster, the fire roared and popped, devouring everything in its path.

Gone. Everything was gone. Her picture of Jarrod, her wedding ring, the home they'd built out of hard work and sweat. The Hoffman family Bible. Even the chest of baby gowns and blankets she'd hand made. All of it gone.

Except her life and her child's life.

In spite of her gratitude for that, a devastating sense of loss weighed her down. Why had God allowed this to happen?

Katie sniffed. She didn't know whether to punch the stranger standing beside her or hug him. If he hadn't come charging into her house like a mad bull, ruining her wedding, her home wouldn't be a burning mess now, and she'd be Mrs. Allan King. Her foggy mind couldn't comprehend how someone as charming as Allan could be wanted by the law.

The stranger stared at her with an unreadable expression. Though fairly young, he looked rugged and tough. His tanned face sported a day or two of whiskers, but his dark hair and eyes reminded her of Uncle Mason's and her brother, Jimmy's. Somehow he'd lost his black western hat and duster, and his hair hung across his collar, too long and unruly to be civilized. She shuddered at his nearness.

Looking past him, she saw Allan on a horse with his hands cuffed in front of him. A sick feeling threatened to upturn her stomach as she realized her dreams were dying. She glanced at the stranger. Her throat hurt from crying and choking on the smoke, but she had to know. "What did Allan do?" Her voice sounded weak and hoarse.

Something flickered in the man's eyes. A muscle in his jaw twitched. "His name's Ed Sloane, not Allan. He's a thief and a murderer, ma'am. You should be thankful we arrived before you married him. You would have lost all you had to that scoundrel."

Katie shivered. Could what he said possibly be the truth? Was Allan really a murderer? She narrowed her eyes, somehow wanting—needing—to blame this man for all her troubles. "Looks to me like that happened anyway."

The man glared back. "Homes can be rebuilt, but people don't come back from the dead." He turned and stormed off.

Katie hiked up her chin. She had never met anyone so rude and insensitive.

A loud crash pulled her gaze back to the fire. The second story collapsed onto the lower floor. Carter ran back and forth, futilely tossing bucket after bucket of water on the flames.

What would she do now? How could she get by without a house?

If not for her child, she might be able to live in the barn's storeroom for a while, but she had the baby to think of—and Carter lived there. She still had a small pittance in the bank; however, that money would have to go to pay the mortgage, or she'd lose her land.

Katie used her sleeve to wipe off her damp face. How could such a beautiful morning so full of hope turn into such a tragedy?

She knew she should be relieved that she had escaped marrying a criminal, but her whole body felt numb as if she were still trapped in the choking smoke.

The stranger stopped to talk with the marshal. Katie glanced around and realized that Sam and the judge were nowhere to be seen.

The marshal trudged her way while the stranger held Allan's horse. He stopped in front of her and removed his hat. "I'm right sorry about your house, Mrs. Hoffman. I didn't mean for this to happen."

Katie wanted to console him, but the words couldn't quite make it past her throat. She'd never met the marshal, though she'd seen him in town.

"Anyway, just be glad you didn't marry that scoundrel. You'd have been sorry, I'm sure."

As the marshal trod off, Carter dropped the bucket he been using to douse the fire beside the trough and turned in her direction. With shoulders sagging, he shuffled forward and stopped a few feet in front of her.

"I'm sorry, Miz Hoff—" His brows dipped. "Uh—it is still Miz Hoffman, isn't it?"

Tears burned her eyes, and she nodded.

"I tried to save the house, ma'am. But it was too far gone after we got your. . .uh, that fellow corralled. What do you reckon he did?"

She shrugged and cleared her throat. "That man"—she nudged her head toward the stranger—"said something about Allan being a thief and a murderer."

Her voice cracked, and Carter glanced at her with sympathetic gray eyes. "If you don't mind me saying so, I never liked that feller much. Can't tell you why, but there was something shifty about him."

Katie glanced down at her throbbing, swelling wrist. She didn't dare move it for fear of feeling that stabbing pain again. "I think deep down I felt that way, too. I was just so desperate that I thought Allan was the answer to my problems."

"I reckon he wasn't." Carter swiped his arm across his forehead. "You need to see the doctor about that arm."

She nodded, dreading the long drive to town. "Could you please hitch the horses?"

"Sure thang. And I'm real sorry about your house, ma'am." He ambled toward the barn.

Katie watched the smoke spiraling up, disturbing a perfectly beautiful autumn sky. How she wished she could just drift away like a cloud, feeling only the warmth of the sun surrounding her instead of this hollowness.

With her good arm, she wiped the tears from her face. She'd cried enough. She'd never been an overly weepy female and wasn't going to start today. Staying angry with the stranger would help.

Right now, she had to make some plans. First was get to town and see the doctor. Then maybe she could stay at the boardinghouse or at the pastor's home a day or two. Somehow, she had to keep her land. Her child's inheritance. It was all she had left to give her baby.

She watched the marshal mount his horse and lead the one carrying Allan away. Funny, Allan was the only thing she didn't regret losing. She should have listened closer to that inner voice filling her with apprehension. But hadn't she thought he was God's answer to her prayers? Somehow, she'd missed hearing God's voice.

The stranger walked toward her, carrying the bucket. He ladled water into the dipper and handed it to her. She took it, surprised at his kindness, and drank like a water-starved woman crossing a desert. When she finished, he carried it back to the well, then filled up a canteen he took off his saddle.

Behind her, horses snorted and a harness jingled. She needed to mentally prepare herself for moving onto the wagon bench. It would hurt—and she couldn't imagine enduring that pain all over. Though her wrist still throbbed, if she sat still, it was bearable. At least her leg wasn't broken where the chair had fallen on it.

The stranger strode toward her again, his hat back on and pulled low on his forehead. She wondered what his story was. He looked more like an outlaw than Allan ever had. The man stopped at the end of the wagon and tied up his black gelding. "What are you doing?" Katie glared at him.

"I'm fixin' to drive you into town to see the doctor." He glowered back, his lips pressed tight in a straight line.

"Carter can drive me."

The man shook his head. "He needs to stay here and make sure the fire doesn't jump across the dirt and ignite your barn and fields."

Katie cast a frantic look toward the barn. She hadn't thought of that. Her cattle needed the hay stored there to make it through the winter. Glancing back at the remains of the house, she could see how the dried grass had burned right up to the dirt line, which had been made by cows and horses moving back and forth to the south pasture.

As much as she didn't want to admit it, he was right.

She closed her eyes, took a steadying breath, and scooted off the end of the wagon. Immediately, her whole body seemed ablaze. Instead of supporting her, the injured leg gave way. Letting go of her wounded arm, she threw out her good arm to break her fall, sending jagged pain charging through her wounded hand and wrist. Before she hit the ground, strong arms pulled her back and scooped her up.

Once again, she rested in the stranger's arms. Too tired and hurt to complain, she laid her head on his shoulder. Maybe she could rest for just a moment.

❧

Dusty carried the woman to the wagon bench and helped her get situated. He wished he had some blankets so she could lie down in back or had a pillow that she could rest her broken wrist on.

He nodded his thanks at the farm hand for hitching up the team. "Keep an eye on those sparks. We don't want to lose the barn."

The man nodded. "I'll get a shovel and throw some dirt on it." He strode back into the barn, looking relieved to be able to do something to help.

The wagon tilted and creaked as Dusty climbed on, and the woman grimaced. He had to admire her spunk. Most women would have fainted dead away after enduring the pain she had when she hopped off the wagon, but she wasn't even crying.

He clucked to her horses and heard a soft moan as the wagon jerked forward. An arrow of guilt pushed its way clear to his heart. This was all his fault. Somehow he had to make it right.

"I. . .uh, I'll stay on and rebuild your house for you."

The woman gasped and looked at him with wide blue

eyes. Her flaxen, smoke-scented hair, probably fixed perfectly before her wedding, now hung in disheveled waves over her shoulders and down to her waist. Would it feel as soft as Emily's had?

Clenching his jaw, he looked away. What kind of an idiot was he, comparing her to Emily and telling her he'd rebuild her house?

"No."

Her single-word response forced him to look back. "No, what?"

She narrowed her eyes, and the nostrils on her cute little nose flared. "I don't want any more of your help. You've done quite enough already."

Dusty clenched his jaw and stared straight ahead, knowing she spoke the truth. His all-consuming quest to see Ed Sloane behind bars had caused him to lose control. This woman had paid the price. He darted a glance at her. Marshal Dodge had told him that Sloane had been wooing a widow woman, but in the mayhem, he'd forgotten what the marshal had called her. "What's your name?"

She stared straight ahead, cradling her injured arm on the top of her big belly. He sure hoped she didn't have her little one before they reached town, because he had no idea how to birth a baby.

"Katie Hoffman." She heaved a sigh as if giving her name was a big effort.

"Dusty McIntyre." He touched the brim of his hat.

They rode the next half hour in silence, but he kept a close eye on Mrs. Hoffman. She looked done in. "If you need to, I don't mind if you lean against my shoulder."

She peeked sideways at him, her eyes wide. With lips

pressed together, she shook her head and looked away.

Dusty sighed. Who could figure out a female? It had taken a lot to offer his shoulder to her, and she just shrugged off his kindness even though she looked exhausted.

He stared ahead, watching the flat, barren landscape of western Oklahoma Territory. He longed for the gently rolling hills of his home in Sanders Creek.

Only he had no home. No job. No family.

He'd spent the last year and a half chasing after Sloane, and now that he'd caught him, Dusty felt empty.

Maybe once Sloane was hanged or in prison, he'd feel satisfied.

Maybe not.

Maybe he should have left vengeance to God. But he hadn't been able to. As long as Sloane was free, good, decent people like Katie Hoffman were in danger of being swindled—or worse. He shuddered to think what would have become of her and her property at the hands of Ed Sloane. He seriously doubted she or her child would have lived very long.

The small town of Claremont came into view on the horizon. As they edged closer, Dusty wondered if such a place would even have a doctor. He glanced at Mrs. Hoffman. Her bobbing head hung down so far it nearly touched her stomach.

Stubborn woman. She could have rested against him if she weren't so thickheaded, but then again, her dignity was about all she had left.

He gently nudged her shoulder, and she glanced up, looking confused. When she moved, pain contorted her pretty face. Her expression cleared as she realized they were in town. "Third house on the right," she spat.

He pulled the team to a stop at the house she'd indicated: a small, wood-frame structure that needed a good paint job. He could only hope the doctor was in better shape than his home.

Dusty lifted Mrs. Hoffman off the wagon and carried her inside, not bothering to knock.

An hour later, the doctor stepped out from behind a white curtain. "Her wrist is broken, and she has a badly bruised leg and hip, not to mention some minor cuts and bruises. Far as I can tell, the baby is fine. You can take her home, but don't let her do anything. For the next few days, she'll feel like she was run down by a herd of cattle. She needs plenty of rest."

Dusty blinked. Didn't the doctor know he wasn't the woman's husband?

The curtain moved, and Mrs. Hoffman hobbled out. He rushed to her side, thinking she shouldn't be walking.

"I don't need your help." She glared at him, daring him to disagree.

He stepped back but stayed close in case she needed him.

"I'll stop back by and pay you, Doc," she said, "after I visit the bank."

The doc waved his hand in the air. "No hurry, ma'am. I'm sure you're good for it."

She took another step, wavered, and then collapsed in the chair Dusty had been sitting in. Her chest rose and fell from her exertion. Holding her arm, now wrapped in stark white plaster of Paris, she peeked up at him.

He knew she didn't want his help but suspected she had no choice. Not making a big deal of things, he bent over and scooped her up. "Where to now?"

"The bank."

Half an hour later, after they'd been to the bank and paid off the doctor, Dusty sat beside Mrs. Hoffman again on the wagon seat.

"What now?" He glanced at her out of the corner of his eye.

She pressed her lips together and looked like she was contemplating things. "Were you serious about offering to help me?"

Dusty nodded, knowing it was the right thing to do.

"All right then. Take me to the pastor's house; then to-morrow you can take me home."

Dusty turned on the seat to face her. "You can't go home. There's no place for you to stay."

She looked at him with pain-filled eyes. "I don't mean the farm. You can take me home to my aunt and uncle's place near Guthrie."

four

Katie turned sideways on the wagon seat, hoping to ease her aching muscles. Just about the time she'd quit hurting from her fall, she and Mr. McIntyre had left Claremont, and now her body ached for a different reason. Someday, someone had to make a comfortable wagon seat.

She'd wanted to leave town the day after the fire, but her stubborn escort had refused. There was wisdom in his decision, not that she'd ever acknowledge it. They had waited three days for her to rest up and make arrangements to sell her cattle. At least her land was secure until next April, when she'd need to make another mortgage payment.

Peeking out the corner of her eye, she studied Dusty McIntyre. He'd been quiet—even distant—rarely talking since they'd left Claremont. But he was always courteous and gentle with her. Who was he, and where had he come from? And who was Allan—no, Ed Sloane—to him?

Taking a deep breath, she put words to her thoughts. "How did you know Ed Sloane, Mr. McIntyre?" The real name of her almost husband left a bitter taste on her tongue.

He glanced at her with those dark-as-midnight eyes peering out from under the western hat that he kept pulled down over his brows. Was that his way of hiding from the world?

"Call me Dusty." A muscle twitched in his shadowed jaw. In a rugged way, he was rather nice-looking. "He was a prisoner in my jail."

"Your jail?"

He nodded. "I used to be the marshal in Sanders Creek."

She blinked, trying to process this new information. How did a man go from being a marshal to a bounty hunter?

"Sloane liked to take advantage of the elderly." He looked her way, a grim set to his lips. "And widows."

Her sudden breath caught in her throat. *Widows?*

Not for the first time in the past few days, guilt washed over her for almost marrying a man without knowing his true character and spiritual condition. She'd assumed Allan believed in God since he had willingly gone to church with her, but that must have been his cunning way of winning her over.

Katie looked down at her hands. She'd ruined everything. If she hadn't agreed to marry Allan—Ed—she'd still have her home, her belongings, and her self-worth. But now she was returning to her aunt and uncle's with her tail tucked between her legs.

Her aunt and uncle would be terribly hurt to learn that she had planned to remarry and hadn't invited them to the wedding. She'd wanted to prove that she was independent and capable of caring for herself.

Now she'd have to face them, carrying a baby she hadn't told them about. Aunt Rebekah had her hands full caring for her four children and her husband. Katie knew if she'd told her about the baby, Rebekah would have found some way to assist her, and Katie hadn't wanted to add more to her aunt's already heavy load.

Katie swallowed the tight lump in her throat. She should have taken her brother, Jimmy, up on his offer and allowed him to help her with the farm. He'd helped her for a month after Jarrod's death, but she'd turned him loose once he got that wandering look in his eyes. If she had encouraged Jimmy to stay, she never would have put her home up for sale or met Allan.

Her stubborn independence had cost her everything. Tears blurred her vision, and she stared out over the dry landscape. The leaves on the few trees in the area had changed to yellow, red, and bright orange. Most of the fields were plowed under, leaving only a few dried stalks exposed. Everything was barren and dying—just like her hopes and dreams.

What would she tell Uncle Mason and Aunt Rebekah? Maybe she could avoid mentioning Allan altogether.

She sighed, and Dusty glanced at her.

"Need another break?"

She shook her head. Could she be any more embarrassed? Having to ask this man to stop nearly every hour so she could relieve herself was so humiliating. She probably shouldn't have even tried traveling, being eight months into her pregnancy, but she didn't have a choice. At least they could make the journey in a day and wouldn't have to camp out overnight.

Katie watched a hawk circle lazily in the sky and wished her life were as carefree. She pressed against the wagon seat, hoping to relieve the ache in her back, and crossed her arms over her stomach. God had deserted her.

First, she'd lost her sweet, loving husband after only four months of marriage.

Now, she'd lost her home and nearly all she owned. She might even have to sell the land she and Jarrod had loved.

Where was God in all this?

She dreaded facing Uncle Mason, who had raised her. He was such a devout Christian man and would be disappointed in her decisions. Still, she longed to be wrapped in his protective arms. He'd comfort her and say that God had a plan—even in this.

Katie hardened her heart and clenched her fists. Well, she wouldn't believe it for a minute. How could losing a husband, a fiancé, and her home possibly be part of God's almighty plan for her?

ﾞﾞ

"Why are you going to your aunt and uncle's instead of your parents' home?"

Katie's surprised blue gaze darted in Dusty's direction. "I lost my parents when I was young, and Uncle Mason and Aunt Rebekah raised my brother, Jimmy, and me."

"Sorry about your parents."

She shrugged. "It's all right. I don't even remember them. I was only three when they died."

What would it be like to lose your parents at such a young age? At least his had lived until he was grown, having died just a year before Emily.

Gripping the reins in his hands, he looked across the heads of the horses pulling the wagon and tried to decide what to do after he dropped off his passenger. The need to compensate her for her loss weighed heavily on him. He'd offered her the hundred-dollar bounty he'd received on Sloane, but she had refused it.

After being a marshal, he hated accepting bounty money, but he'd spent the past year and a half hunting Sloane and capturing several other outlaws in the process. The little money he'd earned had bought food, ammunition, and the other things he'd needed while he was on the trail.

But what should he do now?

A sense of dissatisfaction swirled in his belly. He had

imagined he'd be relishing his victory instead of feeling hollow and empty.

"Vengeance is mine; I will repay, saith the Lord." The scripture his mother often quoted came to mind.

But he was after justice, not vengeance. Wasn't he?

The sun reflected off Mrs. Hoffman's cast, making him wince. It was his fault she was injured, and therefore, it was his responsibility to care for her until she could support herself again. Maybe he could get a job working for her uncle or in the town closest to their farm.

A fly buzzed in his face, and he swatted it. Looking around, he realized they'd arrived at another town. GUTHRIE, CAPITAL OF THE OKLAHOMA TERRITORY read a banner fluttering in the light breeze over Main Street. People strolled up and down the boardwalk, while wagons and riders on horses filled the streets. Two- and three-story brick buildings stood side by side, lining the dirt road. Fragrant smells of fresh-cooked food mingled with the pungent odors of animals and dust.

Katie cleared her throat. "Uncle Mason says on the morning of the land run in 1889 that there was just the rolling hills of the prairie here, but in less than six hours, Guthrie became one of the largest cities west of the Mississippi."

Dusty glanced sideways at her. He'd learned the same information in school but kept silent. This was the most relaxed her voice had sounded since they'd left Claremont. "That a fact?"

"Yes." Her dark blue eyes twinkled, doing funny things to his insides. He focused on a fat old woman dressed in widow's weeds so he wouldn't dwell on how pretty his passenger looked, now that she wasn't scowling.

"Uncle Mason and my pa rode in that first land run. I wish

I could remember more about it. Aunt Rebekah told me that there were thousands of people. She's never seen that many people and horses in one place ever again."

The awe in her voice made him wish he'd experienced the historic event. "So I'm guessing your uncle won some land. You said he lives near Guthrie."

She shook her head and brushed a strand of white gold hair from her eyes. "Actually, my pa won the land, but he signed it over to Uncle Mason."

That seemed odd. Why would a man give away land he'd won fair and square?

"People say my pa was a scoundrel." She pressed her lips together and looked off in the distance as they pulled out of town.

Why would she be attracted to a man like Sloane if her own father had been a rascal? But then, being a scoundrel didn't mean her pa had been a thief or a murderer.

About an hour later, they pulled into a farmyard. A furry brown and white dog barked a greeting and wagged his whole backside. A homey, white, two-story clapboard house with dark green trim stood on a little rise with rolling hills surrounding it. At the bottom of the rise sat a barn with a creek running past.

Beside him, Mrs. Hoffman sighed, probably relieved to have their journey over and to be rid of him. She didn't know it yet, but she wouldn't be rid of him that easily.

A matching pair of dark-haired boys who looked to be five or six years old raced out of the barn and headed straight for the wagon. A man dressed in a plaid shirt and overalls followed them at a slower pace, wiping his hands on a rag. As he drew closer, the man lifted his hat off his forehead and stared at them, a slow smile making him appear younger than Dusty had first thought. Must be her uncle Mason.

The horses snorted and jerked their heads as the boys ran in front of them. Dusty tightened his grip on the reins to keep the animals from bolting. When they settled, he locked the brake in place.

The boys slid to a stop at the same time, scattering dust over their feet. "Who are ya?" the twin on the left asked, wiping his arm across his nose.

"That's Katie." The boy on the right pointed his skinny finger at Dusty's passenger.

"Nuh-uh. You don't know nuthin'." He gave his brother a shove. "Katie's at her farm."

"Is too her." He looked up with big brown eyes that matched his hair. His hand snaked out to pat the wiggling dog at his side. "Ain't you?"

"But she's fat—" The last word echoed on a loud whisper.

Katie sighed and nodded. "These are my twin cousins, Nathan and Nick."

"Ha-ha! Told you so." Nick grinned.

Nathan scowled and crossed his arms over his chest, obviously not happy about being wrong. Dusty bit back a laugh. He imagined the twins could be quite a handful.

"Katie!" The farmer waved and broke into a jog but slowed when his gaze landed on her cast. "What happened?"

She peeked at Dusty, then looked back at her uncle. "It's a long story. This is Dusty McIntyre. He was kind enough to drive me here."

She waved her good hand toward him, though he didn't miss the hint of sarcasm in her voice when she said the word *kind*.

"Dusty, this is my uncle, Mason Danfield."

"Pleasure to meet you, sir." Dusty nodded at Katie's uncle.

"Same here." Mason tipped his hat, and then his gaze landed on his niece's stomach. His surprised gaze darted from her face to her belly and back. His brows dipped. "Why didn't you tell us you were carrying a baby?"

Katie shrugged and eased to her feet. Dusty blinked, stunned that she'd kept her child a secret. Why had she done that?

Mr. Danfield lifted his arms to aid her. She stretched and then pressed her fists into her back. After a moment, she turned to back down the side of the wagon. Dusty held her shoulders and steadied her until Mason had a good hold on her.

"It's so good to have you home again, sweetheart. And just look at you." Mason offered her his arm and shot a curious glance in Dusty's direction. "Rebekah will be so. . .so surprised—and happy."

Feeling a bit left out of the family reunion, Dusty jumped down, dust scattering as his boots hit the ground. He strode to the rear of the wagon to check on his horse.

What would it be like to have a big family? Or any family for that matter? Would he and Emily have children by now if she hadn't died? Shaking off a wave of self-pity, he patted Shadow's muzzle and untied the gelding's reins, then led him to the water trough near the barn. His horse was all the family he needed. Less painful that way.

As he approached the barn, a lean adolescent boy who resembled Katie's uncle walked out carrying a pitchfork. He cast a curious glance at Dusty, nodded a greeting, and then looked toward the wagon. "What's going on, Pa?" Suddenly, the boy's eyes lit up. He leaned the pitchfork against the side of the barn and ran toward the house.

Behind Dusty, a door slammed, and all manner of squeals erupted. He turned to see a brown-haired woman and a young girl hugging Mrs. Hoffman on the porch. Smiles were abundant, and the older woman stared at Mrs. Hoffman's stomach and dabbed at her eyes with the corner of her apron.

"I like a man whose first thought is to care for his animals." The farmer held out his hand. "Call me Mason."

Dusty shook hands, noticing the farmer's firm grip and curious stare.

"Thanks for bringing our Katie home. We didn't expect to see her again until maybe Christmas. And to find out that she's carrying her late husband's child"—he rubbed the back of his neck—"well, that's wonderful news. It'll give her something to remember him by."

Dusty knew the man wondered why he'd brought Katie home, but that was for her to tell.

"You can put your horse in the third stall and give him some oats. I'll unhitch the team and water them."

"Thanks." Dusty nodded, grateful that Mr. Danfield didn't pressure him into explaining. After tending to Shadow, he helped Katie's uncle brush down the team. Together, they walked out of the barn, the setting sun casting long shadows across the ground.

"Did y'all eat?"

Dusty shook his head. Katie hadn't wanted to stop in Guthrie long enough to eat dinner since they were so close to their destination, even though the food she'd packed that morning was long gone.

"We got room for you to stay the night. You planning to head back to Claremont come morning?"

Dusty nearly stumbled but caught himself. How could he explain to this man that he had no plans for tomorrow—or the next day for that matter—other than trying to repay Mrs. Hoffman for all the trouble he'd caused her? He stopped and studied the ground for a moment, trying to decide how much to say.

Mr. Danfield slowed, halted his steps, and waited.

Finally, Dusty looked up. "I want you to know that I'm responsible for Mrs. Hoffman getting hurt. I never meant for it to happen, but it did—and there's more. I'd explain it to you, but I feel she needs to do that. Maybe we can talk after she tells you what happened."

Katie's uncle looked to be sizing him up. The man stood only an inch or so shorter than Dusty, but the breadth of his shoulders was wider, probably from working his land for years. Mason nodded. Dusty waited for him to say something with that slow Southern drawl, but he turned and jogged up the stairs. Not knowing what else to do, Dusty followed.

For some reason, he liked Mason Danfield. There was a quality to the man. And the fact that he hadn't needled Dusty about how Katie had gotten hurt helped set him at ease. He half expected the man to grab him and shove him against the barn until Dusty confessed his part in the event.

The screen door slammed shut as they stepped inside the cozy home. Dusty could hear women's voices chattering like a bunch of magpies and dishes clinking in a room down the hall. The twins raced from room to room, whooping like Indians and merely slowed their pace when their father scolded them. Everywhere Dusty looked were signs of a happy family, making him feel his loss even more. He'd gotten over the deep, aching pain of losing Emily and his home, but he doubted he'd ever forget what he'd lost.

He didn't understand this overwhelming need to protect and care for Katie Hoffman. She didn't belong to him—and probably would be happy to never see him again. Maybe guilt was motivating him.

He removed his hat and hung it on a hook near the front door like Mr. Danfield had done. Dusty needed to figure out what to do next. After spending a year and a half on Sloane's trail, he wanted to settle down, and he had to somehow learn to live a normal life again. For now, Katie Hoffman was part of that life, whether she liked it or not.

five

Katie yawned and stretched, then opened her eyes. The sun glistened in her window from a high angle, and she realized her family had let her sleep in. She knew she ought to feel guilty, but she was too worn out to worry about it.

The babe in her womb flip-flopped as if it, too, had just awakened. She rubbed her hand across her stomach, wondering how many more days would pass before she would be a mother. Would she handle the birthing as well as Rebekah had? She shuddered, not wanting to think of that scary but exciting event. She knew birthing would be painful, but the joy of seeing her child for the first time would give her the strength she would need.

Lying on her side, she studied her brother's sparse room but failed to notice much change. Excitement tickled her insides as she thought about seeing Jimmy again. The last time she had seen her brother was after Jarrod's funeral, when he stayed on to help her for a while.

Katie lumbered up until she sat on the edge of the bed. How did women bear children when they had a whole passel of young 'uns to care for?

Her stomach grumbled, reminding her that she'd skipped breakfast. She slipped off her gown, washed in the water basin, and dressed, grateful for the button-up front of her blue gingham that enabled her to dress herself, even though one hand was in a cast. The sound of deep masculine voices pulled her to the window as she ran the brush through her hair.

Jimmy!

Her eyes drank in the sight of her brother. Though he was four years older than she, they had always been close, and she'd missed him terribly when he'd gone to fight in the Spanish-American War several years ago. Mason had told her last night that Jimmy had gone to Guthrie to pick up supplies and had probably stayed overnight. She'd laughed and wondered if she'd driven straight past him as she and Dusty had ridden through town.

When she saw Dusty, her heart gave a rebellious jump, and she scowled as she watched him shake Jimmy's hand. If a person didn't know better, they might think the two men were brothers, with their matching black hair and eyes and similar build. But her sweet brother was nothing like the man who'd ruined her life, no matter how good-looking that man might be.

With the window closed, she couldn't hear what they were saying. Turning, she bypassed her shoes and plodded barefoot down the stairs.

" 'Bout time you woke up, sleepyhead." Her cousin Deborah's eyes glinted with humor.

Katie reached out and tweaked her nose. "You're getting taller, Deb."

"I am?" The twelve-year-old stretched up on her tiptoes and hugged Katie around the neck. "How's Junior today?"

"Hungry!" Katie laughed with her cousin and took her arm. "But first, I want to see Jimmy."

The front door groaned as Deborah pulled it open. The men stopped talking and turned in their direction.

"Katie!" Jimmy left Dusty and jogged up the porch steps. "Whoa! Look at you."

A nervous giggle escaped her as her brother stared at her huge stomach. She smacked him on the arm. "Give me a hug, you big galoot."

Deborah laughed as she hopped off the end of the porch and disappeared around the side of the house.

Jimmy stepped forward, arms opened, but then stopped. His dark brows furrowed. "Just how am I supposed to do that?"

Katie smiled and shook her head at his teasing. "Just lean over." She grabbed him by the shirt and tugged him down so she could wrap her arms around his neck. Over his shoulder, she caught Dusty coolly watching them. When she met his gaze, one corner of his mouth quirked up in a roguish grin. Her stomach lurched—probably because she hadn't eaten anything yet.

"Good night, sis, you're as big as a—"

She cupped her hand over her brother's mouth. "Don't you say a word, if you know what's good for you."

Jimmy's black eyes glimmered with mischief. Oh, how she'd missed him.

"C'mon in and have some coffee with me."

"Can't. Gotta unload the wagon. Dusty's gonna help." Jimmy adjusted his hat. "We can talk later. Work won't keep."

Jimmy bounded down the stairs and walked past Dusty toward the loaded wagon that sat outside the barn. She was glad he was back home. He'd been restless the past few years. Couldn't seem to find a place to settle. He'd stay home a couple of months, then ride out again as if he were searching for something—or someone.

Instead of following Jimmy, Dusty ambled toward Katie, making her heart skip a beat. She wanted to dart back inside, but a woman her size didn't do much darting. She lifted her chin and held her ground, ignoring her swirling stomach.

"Mornin'." Dusty yanked off his hat and held it in front of him, leaving his black hair in need of straightening. "How you feeling today? I know yesterday's ride couldn't have been easy on you."

Katie blinked, taken off guard by the concern she saw in his onyx eyes. "I'm doing fine. Thank you."

He smiled and donned his hat. "That's good. You look more rested than you did yesterday. Well, I'd better go help your brother."

He turned and sauntered to the wagon, his long-legged gait eating up the ground in quick order. She narrowed her gaze. Why did he have to be nice to her? It made blaming him for her troubles that much harder. Her stomach gurgled, and she went back inside.

As Katie entered the kitchen, Aunt Rebekah glanced up from the worktable where she was sitting, making dinner rolls. Her blue eyes lit up, and she smiled. "Feeling better?"

"Yes, but I desperately need some food—and some coffee." Katie poured herself a cup, then pulled out a chair and sat down.

"I saved you some breakfast." Rebekah wiped her flour-coated hands on her apron, stood, and crossed the room to the stove.

"Why is Mr. McIntyre still here? I figured he'd head out early this morning." Katie closed her eyes and savored the coffee as it slid down her throat and warmed her belly.

"He told Mason he thought he'd stay in the area. Maybe look for work in Guthrie."

Katie froze, her mouth agape, as disappointment surged

through her. Of all the places Dusty McIntyre could settle, why did he have to pick Guthrie?

Rebekah set the plate in front of her, and the scent of fresh biscuits, bacon, and eggs wafted up. "Mmm. Smells wonderful. I'm just glad I can eat eggs now. When I was first carrying, I couldn't stand to see or smell them."

"I know just what you mean. About all I could stomach those first months were grits and oatmeal." Smiling, Rebekah sat back down, pinched off a section of dough, and rolled it into a ball. "He seems like a nice man to me."

"Who?" Katie slathered butter and plum jam onto her biscuit, then stuffed a huge bite into her mouth.

"Mr. McIntyre." Rebekah set her hands in her lap and stared off in the distance. "He reminds me of Mason when I first met him. He has that same haunted, hurting look. I wonder if he lost someone he loved."

"I don't know. He doesn't talk all that much." She forked some eggs into her mouth, wishing Rebekah would change the subject.

"So, are you going to tell me why you came to visit so unexpectedly?"

Maybe changing the subject wasn't the greatest idea.

"Is it because of the baby or because you got hurt?" Rebekah glanced at Katie's arm.

"Not exactly. It's a long story."

"I've got all day. Or would you prefer Mason was here when you talk about it? He didn't want to push you last night because you looked so tired."

Katie pushed her eggs around on her plate. Suddenly, they didn't taste so good. She closed her eyes and sighed, knowing she couldn't keep the truth from her aunt.

She told Rebekah how she'd met Allan and how he had swept her off her feet with his charm and persistence, even going to church with her. After taking a swig of coffee to steady her nerves, she told her aunt about the wedding and about Dusty storming in and Allan pushing her down and running away. Rebekah's eyes widened, and her hand lifted to cover her mouth as Katie told her about the house catching on fire and Dusty rescuing her.

Rebekah reached her flour-coated hand across the table and laid it on Katie's arm. "I'm so sorry about your home, sweetheart. So, Mr. McIntyre saved your life? Remind me to give that man a hug."

Eyes moist at the memory of her loss, Katie sputtered and her back stiffened. "Well, yes, he saved me, but he's also responsible for ruining my wedding and burning down my house."

Rebekah's mouth quirked to one side, and her brows lifted in disbelief. "Sounds to me like he kept you from making a terrible mistake, besides saving your life—and your child's."

"Yes, but. . ." Katie considered her aunt's words. Aunt Rebekah had a way of putting everything in its proper perspective.

"No buts. I know you, Katie. You've always needed someone to blame when things go wrong. From what you've told me, Mr. McIntyre wasn't even in the house when the lamp was knocked over, so it couldn't be his fault."

A door banged, and the twins stormed into the kitchen. "We're starved, Mama," they said in unison.

Rebekah smiled. "Are you now? Well, perhaps I could find a cookie to hold you over until dinner."

The twins' eyes gleamed, and they nodded their heads.

Grateful for the reprieve, Katie closed her eyes as her aunt stood. She wasn't ready to let go of her anger, even though she knew that's what God wanted her to do. For some reason, she needed to stay angry at Dusty. Was she afraid if she didn't that she might just discover she liked him?

Even though she dearly loved her aunt and uncle, Katie didn't want to live in their home again. Her independence was too important to her.

Considering her options, she nibbled a piece of bacon and watched her aunt, who'd returned to making her dinner rolls. She could sell her farm and would have the money to get a small house somewhere, maybe in Guthrie. She'd be closer to her family and still be living on her own. But then her child would have no inheritance, and she'd feel as if she had failed Jarrod.

She had to do something. Having lost her mother and father when she was just a tiny girl, she'd always felt something was missing. Oh, Uncle Mason and Aunt Rebekah had loved her as much as real parents, but she'd always wondered what things would have been like if her parents had lived.

She shook that thought away. For now, she'd keep the ranch and find some other means of support, like sewing. Though it would be difficult with the cast, she could manage. Maybe she could get Jimmy to drive her back to town so she could scout out her options.

She stared into her coffee cup and swirled the black liquid. One thing was for sure: She was done with men. She couldn't stand the pain of loving and losing again—or being taken in by another con man. No, she'd find some work and raise her child without a man's help.

❧

Dusty patted Shadow's rump and walked out of the livery. While his horse received a new pair of shoes, he needed to find some work. The livery owner didn't need any help but thought that the man at the mercantile might. Dusty clenched his jaw. Working in a store wasn't exactly his area of expertise, but if it would enable him to fulfill his obligation to Mrs. Hoffman, he could do it for a time.

As he stepped inside the mercantile, he paused to allow his eyes to adjust to the dim lighting. All manner of scents tickled his nose, from leather, to spices, to the pickle barrel at his side. His mouth watered at the thought of eating a juicy pickle, but he was here on business, not for a snack.

A heavyset woman behind the counter smiled. "Good morning. What can I help you with?"

Dusty looked around, hoping to speak with her husband, but no one else was in the store. He removed his hat and plodded toward the counter, his boots echoing on the wooden floor planks. "Morning, ma'am. Your husband around?"

She shook her head, and wisps of curly gray hair danced around her wrinkled face. "No. He had to pick up some orders at the train depot. I can help you with 'bout anything he could."

Dusty cleared his throat. "The truth is, I'm looking for work."

"Oh." Her gaze took him in from top to bottom.

He figured he looked more like an outlaw to her than a store clerk. "I can assure you that I'm honest and trustworthy. Mason Danfield will vouch for me."

"Oh, well, that's good. Mr. Danfield is a fine judge of character. But the truth is, we just hired a man last week. We needed someone to make deliveries. I'm truly sorry."

Her compassionate gaze soothed Dusty's disappointment. He looked around the store, and his eyes landed on a colorful sign advertising soda pop. "I'd like to try one of those." He pointed at the sign.

The woman smiled. "Those new soft drinks are quite the rage now." She moved to the back of the store and returned with a small bottle. Using an opener, she flipped off the top, and a hissing sound erupted.

Dusty took the cold bottle and laid a coin on the counter. He took a sniff of the sweet-smelling drink, then a taste. Fizzy bubbles tickled his tongue, but the drink was cool and refreshing. Much better than the lukewarm, metallic-tasting water in his canteen. He swigged down the drink in three swallows and contemplated getting another. Maybe later. He clunked the bottle onto the counter. "Thank you. I may be back later for some supplies." Dusty tipped his hat at her and licked the remaining sweetness off his lips.

"We'll be here, and we're glad to help." She smiled and waved, making Dusty wish he had a grandmother alive somewhere.

He stepped outside and blinked against the brightness as his boots clunked on the boardwalk. Guthrie was an active town. A number of men and several women moseyed along the sides of the street, stopping at different establishments.

He'd heard that Guthrie was one of the most progressive towns west of the Mississippi. One building even had an underground area for storing buggies and stabling horses for the people who worked there.

Sanders Creek was a far cry from Guthrie. Dusty reckoned the town had a new marshal by now—maybe Tom. Even though he'd never formally quit, he'd been gone more than a year and a half. He scowled, not wanting to think of his hometown and all he'd lost there.

Looking at Guthrie again, he remembered the stories Mason and Jimmy had told him. When they first came here, shortly before the first Oklahoma land rush, thousands of people lived here in tents and covered wagons. Dusty tried to imagine the scene.

As he stood in front of the mercantile, leaning against a post, two young women dressed in frilly gowns and carrying parasols crossed the dirt street and walked in his direction. They giggled and talked behind their hands, leaning close to speak in one another's ears. Something told him they were talking about him. He glanced down at his denim pants. A streak of dirt lined one leg where he had leaned Shadow's hoof as he checked the shoe earlier this morning.

The women neared the steps next to him and stopped at the bottom. The cute brunette cleared her throat, making him realize they were waiting for his assistance. He pushed away from the pole and held out his hand. The brunette batted her lashes at him, and a coy smile tugged at her pretty lips. Dusty helped her up the steps, then turned to aid her friend, a shy auburn-haired gal. After he assisted her, the two ambled on their way, giggling and looking back over their shoulders at him.

He jogged down the steps and crossed the street, heading toward the marshal's office. Why hadn't their attention affected him? He ought to consider it a compliment, but his thoughts kept traveling back to Katie Hoffman's dark blue gaze glaring at him. She obviously couldn't be rid of him quick enough, but something inside him wished she felt differently.

Dusty nearly stumbled as the realization hit him—he liked her. For some odd reason, he felt an attraction to the prickly woman. Oh, sure she was pretty enough with that mass of golden hair and those simmering eyes, even though she was with child.

He'd always been drawn to needy people. Maybe that's why he liked his job as marshal, because it allowed him to help those in need. As he looked up, his gaze landed on a sign indicating the marshal's office, and he headed that way.

The door rattled as he entered, and a lean man sitting behind the desk looked up. The small office smelled of cigar smoke and gun oil.

"Howdy, stranger. What can I do for you?" The man leaned back in his chair, surveying Dusty as if he expected trouble.

Hoping to put the man at ease, Dusty crossed the room and held out his hand. "Dusty McIntyre. I drove Katie Hoffman from her farm in Claremont to her uncle's farm."

"I'm Homer White." The marshal stood and shook Dusty's hand. "McIntyre, huh? That name sounds familiar. You're not wanted for something, are you?"

Dusty could tell the man was partly serious with his question. "I was marshal in Sanders Creek a few years back."

Marshal White's eyes narrowed as if he was searching his mind for a memory. Suddenly, his gray eyes widened. "Oh, you're that McIntyre. Sorry to hear about your wife and home. D'you ever catch the man that caused all your troubles?"

Dusty nodded. "Just did." He glanced around the room. "I was hoping to take a look at your WANTED posters. Now that Ed Sloane is locked up, I need to find something else to do."

A drawer squeaked on the desk as the marshal pulled it open. He took out a stack of papers and flopped them on the desk. "Have at it."

Dusty thumbed through the stack, recognizing several faces. He handed one to the marshal. "That man's in jail in

Enid. Caught him last month."

Marshal White nodded. "Glad to know that. I'll put his poster in my CAPTURED file." He opened the bottom drawer of his desk and slid the paper inside.

Dusty smiled and studied some more posters. The problem was, if he went after another outlaw, he wouldn't be able to stay around and help Mrs. Hoffman. He sighed. What he needed was a job in town.

"You're welcome to have a seat. I don't get too much company—unless there's trouble."

Dusty nodded his thanks and sat down. "You know of any honest work around here? I'd kind of like to stick around these parts for a while."

The marshal grinned, showing his yellowed teeth. "That Katie Hoffman is a fine-looking woman, isn't she?" His expression sobered. "Heard tell she lost that young husband of hers. Downright shame. They weren't married but a few months."

Dusty stared out the window. Was his attraction to Katie that obvious?

"Tell you what. I could use a deputy. The one I had left town a few weeks ago when he got word his father was dying. You interested?"

Dusty's gaze darted back to the marshal. The man was serious. Dusty studied the dirt on the wood floor. Was he ready to pin on a badge again?

"I know what you're thinking, young man. Wondering if you still have it in you after getting gut shot like you did back in Sanders Creek." The man leaned back in his chair with his hands crossed behind his head. "Best thing to do is get back on the horse once you've been thrown."

Dusty knew it was the truth, but sometimes climbing back on wasn't easy.

"You got a place to stay?"

Dusty shook his head. "Not yet."

"Good. You can stay with me. I live by myself. Got a spare bedroom and a place out back to stable your horse—assuming you've got one. And I'll pay you seventy-five dollars a month, just like I did the other fellow."

Dusty blinked. Rarely in his life had things come so easily. He waited for the *however*—but it never came. He reached out his hand. "Marshal, you've got yourself a deputy."

six

Katie brushed her damp hair and paced the length of the porch and back. She desperately needed to find some way to get to town. Uncle Mason was too busy to take her, and Jimmy had gone down to Texas to scout out some cattle. She would ask her cousin Josh but didn't want to get the fourteen-year-old in trouble with his father.

A sharp pain forced her to take a seat in the nearby rocking chair. She rubbed at a spot on her upper leg where the babe tended to sit on a nerve, sending sharp stabs into her hip and down her leg. How in the world had Rebekah managed to do this five times? A picture of two small graves on the hill behind the house reminded her to be thankful for her active child. She remembered the gripping pain when Rebekah's third child had been stillborn and the horrible shock when Mason and Rebekah woke up one morning to discover their youngest daughter dead in her cradle at only five months old.

No matter how much discomfort her babe caused, Katie was determined not to complain. If not for Dusty McIntyre, she could have lost her child.

Katie shook her head, not wanting to think of being beholden to the handsome bounty hunter. A man like that was a loner, destined to travel the countryside, ever in search of his prey. It must be lonely. What would drive a man to want to live such a solitary life?

Besides, he was gone now. He'd ridden out nearly a week

ago and hadn't returned. At least her anger had cooled somewhat, not having to be around him daily.

She stood, rubbing her back. There had to be some way she could get to town. Perhaps the dress-shop owner could use some help. Katie had mastered her sewing skills by helping her aunt make clothes for their big family and surely would be an asset to a dressmaker, even though it would take her much longer to sew with the cast on.

The porch thudded as the twins charged up the steps. She loved her young cousins, but they just about wore everyone out with their active natures. They stopped running but still bounced around her.

"Nathan says you swallowed a punkin. That true?" Nick stared up at her, his brown eyes wide. Nathan elbowed Nick in the side, but he didn't look away.

Katie's cheeks warmed as she considered how to respond. The door behind her squealed open, and Rebekah stepped outside.

"There you are. You boys wash up and wait for me in the parlor. It's time for your reading lesson."

"Aw, Ma. Why do we have to learn readin'?" Nathan's shoulders sagged.

"Yeah, we ain't never even been to school yet." Nick glanced at his brother and took a similar posture.

Katie tucked her lips together to keep from laughing.

"I'm determined for you to start school already knowing your alphabet." Rebekah stared down at the boys, her hands on her hips. "Now go inside."

"Aww," the boys whined in unison.

Rebekah grinned and shook her head. "Katie, are you doing all right?"

"Yes, but I'm so bored that I asked Deborah to help me wash my hair—and it's not even Saturday. I want to ride into town and see if that new dressmaker needs some help."

Her aunt's eyes widened. "You'll do no such thing. A woman in your condition has no business traveling. You risk doing injury to your child, not to mention tiring yourself out."

Katie heaved a deep breath. "I did fine on the trip from Claremont. Besides, I need to get work so I can start saving money to rebuild my house and make my next mortgage payment."

Rebekah laid her hand on Katie's arm. "Sweetheart, don't worry about that now. You have a home here for as long as you want. We love having you here."

Inside the house, Katie heard the sound of breaking glass. Rebekah yanked her hand back and spun around, hurrying inside. "Don't stay outside so long that you catch cold," she called over her shoulder as she shut the door.

Katie sighed. Nobody understood how she felt. She loved her family, but after being on her own, she craved her independence. She wanted her cozy home back.

A gentle autumn breeze tickled her cheek and sent leaves from the nearby oak tree spiraling to the ground. Summers might be hot in the Oklahoma Territory, but autumn was wonderful with the cooler yet comfortable temperatures.

She stared off in the distance, wondering how she could get to town. Rebekah didn't understand her driving need for independence. And why all the fuss? Riding to Guthrie didn't take nearly as long as the trip from Claremont had taken, and she'd managed to travel that distance just fine. Well, maybe not fine, but she'd made it.

She'd have to keep thinking on it. Uncle Mason would tell

her to pray, but God had let her down. He hadn't saved her home or kept her from breaking her wrist.

Emotions swirled through her. She knew it was wrong to blame God. Bad things happened in life, like Jarrod's accident and the fire. She'd drive herself crazy trying to sort it all out. Uncle Mason believed there was a purpose for everything that happened in life, and she thought she believed that also—until so many bad things occurred.

She looked up at the beautiful sky. She knew in her heart that God was in control and cared for His people, but she needed her mind to align with her heart.

A horse's whinny drew her attention to the road coming from town. She narrowed her eyes and placed her hand on her brow to block the sun as she tried to see if she knew the rider on the dark horse.

Her heart flip-flopped. Dusty McIntyre had returned.

Hope surged through her body, making her limbs tremble. Dusty had said he'd do anything he could to help her. Perhaps she could get him to take her to town.

≈

As Dusty rode up to the Danfield farm, he had a strange sense of coming home. Katie stood on the porch, leaning against the railing, as if waiting for him. Her long, damp hair hung down to her waist, drying in the light breeze like the flaxen mane of a wild mustang. Tingling sparks shot through his body, making him wish he had the right to run his hands through her hair.

Other than when he met Emily, he'd never cared if a woman favored him or not. But for some reason, he wanted Katie to be partial to him. Maybe it would assure him that she'd forgiven him for the trouble he'd caused her.

He nudged Shadow into a trot and quickly ate up the distance separating him and Katie. After hopping off his horse, he tied the gelding to the porch railing and climbed the steps. Katie now sat in a rocking chair with her hair behind her.

Dusty yanked off his hat, feeling a bit shy in her presence. He was never sure whether she'd be pleasant or bite his head off. Marshal White had told him that women were often extra-emotional when they were carrying. At least that had been the marshal's experience with his wife.

"Afternoon. Why don't you have a seat?" Katie waved her hand toward the other rocking chair.

He hesitated a moment, taken off guard by the kindness in her voice. As he passed her, he tried not to notice that her middle looked even bigger than it had last week. He averted his gaze but wondered how a body could stretch so much.

"I didn't expect to see you again." She laced her fingers and rested her hands across her big belly.

Dusty rolled the brim of his hat, not used to making small talk. He'd been alone for so long that he figured he wasn't the best of company.

"Aunt Rebekah said you thought you might settle in Guthrie."

He nodded and glanced her way, trying not to notice how pretty she looked when she wasn't scowling. "I took a job as deputy marshal." He didn't think it proper to tell her he was rooming with Marshal White.

"That's good. I'm sure the marshal was delighted to be able to hire someone with your experience and capabilities."

Dusty wanted to allow his chest to swell with pride at her first compliment, but too many years of chasing crooks had taught him that when someone was handing out favors, it was usually because they desired something. Disappointed, he sat back in his chair and faced the barn instead of Katie. Was it too much to hope she might actually like him? What was it she wanted?

"So, did you come out to see Uncle Mason?"

"No, I rode out to check on you."

"Me? Why would you feel that's necessary? Uncle Mason and Aunt Rebekah are quite able to care for me, not that I need them to."

Dusty darted a glance in her direction. Her cute little chin was lifted in the air as if he'd greatly offended her, and her eyes sparked with indignation. She reminded him of a fancy hen strutting around the barnyard.

"I intend to make sure you're all right and to figure out a way to make up for the pain I've caused you."

She peered at him, both curiosity and anger flashing in her eyes. "I don't need you to take care of me." She pushed herself up. "That's the whole problem. I want to care for myself, but everyone seems bent on doing it for me." Turning away, she awkwardly crossed her arms over her stomach.

Dusty stood and walked over to stand behind Katie. Her hair fell in golden waves, teasing him to reach out and run his fingers through it. He jerked his hand back as he came to his senses. This woman wouldn't appreciate his advances.

Suddenly, she spun around. "There is one thing you could do for me, if you're serious about helping me."

Dusty held his breath as he studied her face. Her tanned complexion was much prettier and more natural than that of pale-faced city women who hid from the sun. Up close, her sapphire eyes had flecks of gray and several shades of blue. A smattering of soft freckles dotted her small nose, giving her a spunky, carefree look.

He knew he should be suspicious of her quick turnabout, but his mouth had suddenly gone too dry for him to respond.

She stepped closer, laying her uninjured hand on his arm. Goose bumps erupted at her touch, making him feel like a giddy schoolboy. He glanced at her lips, wishing he had the right to kiss them.

Katie stared up at him, as if she, too, were caught up in the magic of the moment. Was it possible she had some feelings for him? Why did he even care?

Katie cleared her throat, blinked her thick lashes, and took a step back. "I. . .uh. . .need to get to town. Uncle Mason is busy, and Jimmy's gone. Could you possibly take me?"

Dusty stepped back and turned away, disappointed that her attentions had only been a ploy to get him to help her. He remembered Rebekah's comment that Katie shouldn't have traveled to their ranch in her condition. It could be bad for the baby. Well, he wouldn't be part of causing her more pain. If he drove her to town and something happened to the baby, she'd just have another thing to blame him for, and he'd never forgive himself.

He faced her again. "I'm sorry, but I can't do that."

Katie hiked up her chin again. "Can't? Or won't?"

"You've got no business traveling to town in your"—he waved his hand toward her stomach—"condition." Dusty was certain his ears were bright red.

Katie glared at him. "You're just like the rest of them—wanting to keep me tied here to the ranch. All I want is a chance to talk to the dressmaker to see if she needs any help. I want to support myself and my child, not live off my relatives."

He could understand her frustration, but she had a baby to worry about. "All you need to be thinking about right now is your child. The rest you can worry about later."

She crossed her arms over her chest, the cast on her wrist reminding him once again of the pain he'd caused.

Katie dipped her brows, her eyes taking on a stormy glare. "What would you know about it? I lost my husband after only four months of marriage, my home, and everything I owned except my land. There's no way this side of heaven you could know how I feel."

Dusty closed his eyes and waited for the thunderstorm of pain and anger to subside. His stomach ached as if he'd been sucker punched when he wasn't looking. He narrowed his gaze and took hold of Katie's upper arms. Her eyes widened in surprise and apprehension. "Oh, I know how you feel all right. The difference is, you have a child to remember your husband by, but I've got nothing."

He released her, ignoring the curiosity and repentance he saw in her gaze. He ran down the stairs, jumped onto Shadow, and rode off, hoping he'd never see Katie Hoffman again. He was done trying to please that persnickety woman.

seven

Dusty kicked Shadow into a gallop. Katie had no way of knowing how closely their losses were related. The difference was he bore his alone, while she had a whole houseful of people to help her, even if she didn't want their help.

Even God had deserted him.

No, that wasn't fair. He was the one who'd run off and left God behind when he was aching over Emily's death. If only he knew how to find his way back.

But it was too late for him.

He eased Shadow to a trot, sorry for taking his frustration out on his trusted steed.

Had there ever been a more stubborn woman than Katie Hoffman?

The wind suddenly whipped out of the north, bringing with it colder temperatures and a threat of snow, which chilled his bones after the warm weather of the past week. It never ceased to amaze him how quickly the weather could change here. Though it was a bit early for snow, in Oklahoma, anything could happen weatherwise. Dusty reined Shadow to a halt, dismounted, and untied his duster from behind his saddle. He shrugged into the long, brown coat, leaving it open and billowing around his legs.

He studied the yellowed rolling hills. Some leaves still stubbornly clung to the trees, but in another month they'd be gone. He had never cared too much for winter and the hardships it brought.

Dusty sighed, wrestling with his feeling of unease. He'd thought after capturing Ed Sloane he would be content and could finally put his past behind him. Instead, he felt like something was missing in his life. Was it that he no longer had a goal? Had he been focused so long on capturing Sloane that he couldn't settle down and live a normal life?

Shadow nickered, and Dusty tugged on the reins, pulling his horse closer. He patted the gelding's soft muzzle.

He didn't want to admit it, but he was jealous of Mason Danfield. Mason had a loving family, a nice home, and his heart was right with God. Maybe this restlessness in him had more to do with his walking away from God than capturing Sloane.

Dusty pressed down his hat, mounted Shadow, and urged the horse into a trot. His parents had been God-fearing people and raised him to be that way. But when things turned bad, he had ridden away from his friends and from God, preferring to suffer alone.

Was it possible for God to forgive a man who had hardened his heart against Him?

Dusty shook his head. No, he had to face facts. He'd blown his chance with God. There was nothing else left but to endure the rest of his life the best he could.

He thought about Katie. It was obvious she wanted nothing to do with him, unless he was willing to do things her way. That shouldn't bother him, but it did.

He had to admire her stubborn desire for independence. Most women in her shoes would be satisfied to sit back and allow their family to take them in. But not Katie.

As he rode toward town, he considered how he might help

her regain her independence. He wouldn't bring her to town like she requested, but there had to be something he could do.

A strong gust of wind blew, chilling his belly. Lowering his eyes, he noticed the spot where he'd torn off a button when his shirt had snagged on the chair this morning. He shouldn't have worn it this way, but his only other shirt was dirty. He'd traveled light when he was on the road, taking only one change of clothing. He would find a place and wash his dirty things, trading back and forth, but now that he had a town job and needed the respect of the people, he figured he ought to get some new clothes.

He sighed and thought of the store-bought clothes he'd had in the past. The problem was, being tall with long arms, he had trouble finding shirts with sleeves that fit comfortably. He much preferred custom-made shirts. As he rode into Guthrie, he scanned the signs for a tailor. It would be a good idea to get some made.

As if one of those newfangled electric lights had lit up in his mind, an idea started forming. A plan to help Katie and himself. He turned Shadow around and headed back to the mercantile.

Yep, he had just the idea that would help her take the first step to regain her independence.

&

"Aunt Rebekah, you need to let me help you more." Katie dropped into the kitchen chair and watched her aunt and cousin washing the dishes. She'd cleaned off the table but didn't want to admit the going back and forth had winded her.

"You do plenty around here. You need to take it easy these last weeks and save your strength for the birthing."

Katie wanted to ask Rebekah just what was involved with

that, but with Deborah in the room, she held her tongue.

Josh sauntered in, reminding her of her brother when he was fourteen. Tall, lanky, three-fourths man and one-fourth boy. Josh's hair more closely resembled Rebekah's medium brown than Mason's black hair, but his features were more like his father's.

"Pa said for me to get the food scraps for the hogs."

Rebekah nodded her head toward the wooden bucket that held the vegetable scraps. Josh grabbed the pail and hurried out, looking uncomfortable in the women's domain.

"There's something I've been meaning to show you." Rebekah wiped her hands on a towel. "Deb, after you finish rinsing, dump the water on the green beans and join Katie and me in my room."

"Yes, ma'am." Deborah gave a smile that looked much like her mother's.

It was interesting how Deborah had her father's dark coloring, but her features more resembled her mother's, just the opposite of Josh. Would Katie's baby be a combination of her and Jarrod, or would it favor one side of the family more than the other? Katie stuck her little finger down the end of her cast and rubbed her itching arm as she followed Rebekah to her bedroom. Warm memories flashed through her mind of tiptoeing into her aunt and uncle's bedroom with Jimmy and the other children and waking up Mason and Rebekah early on Christmas morning. As she glanced around, she noticed a new Flying Geese–patterned quilt covered the bed and curtains from a matching fabric hung from the window.

At the foot of the bed was an old trunk. Her aunt lifted the latch, and Katie peered over Rebekah's shoulder to see what was inside. Her heart leaped when she saw the folded stacks of baby gowns, diapers, and blankets. That was another reason she needed to get to town—to get fabric to make some baby clothes.

Rebekah lifted a pale pink flannel gown and caressed it. "I made this for Susanna right after she was born. The twins pretty much wore out the clothing I had saved from the other children, so I needed new things for Sus—"

"I'm sorry, Aunt Rebekah." Katie laid her hand on her aunt's shoulder. "I never considered how my being here would stir up old memories or make things harder for you."

Rebekah dotted her eyes. "No, I'm sorry. It's just that I haven't looked at these things since I put them away after Susanna's death. It was too painful at first, but it's good for me now. God has healed my pain, though I still miss my baby girl."

"I know. I miss Jarrod, too, but the pain of his loss isn't as sharp as it was at first."

Rebekah hugged Katie. "Yes, God's grace softens the ache of losing those we love because we know we'll see them again in heaven."

Katie wanted to believe that—knew it was true. She needed to forgive God—and Dusty—but she didn't know how.

"Look at this! Oh, I hope you have a girl. My friends gave me so many darling things after I had Susanna." She held up a tiny mint green cotton dress with smocking across the chest and flowers embroidered over it.

"Oh, how precious! That dress almost makes me want a girl, though I have to be honest. I'm hoping for a son to carry on the Hoffman name."

"I don't blame you. Mason was so excited our first child was a boy. Do you remember? You were only five back then."

Katie shook her head, reached in the trunk, and picked up a soft, crocheted blanket. "No, I don't remember his reaction, just that I wanted to hold Josh all the time."

Rebekah dug farther down in the stack of clothes and pulled out a long, white, lacy gown. "All my children were dedicated to God in this. It would make me so happy if you were to have your child dedicated in it."

Katie blinked. She hadn't even thought about that. Could she dedicate their child to the Lord if she was still angry with Him?

"You are planning to have your child dedicated, aren't you?"

Katie looked at her aunt. "I hadn't even thought about it until you mentioned it."

Rebecca glanced down and fingered a pastel blue blanket. "Katie, are you letting your grief build a wall between you and God?"

She heard the concern in her aunt's voice and nodded her head.

Rebekah put her arm around Katie's shoulders. "I can't pretend to know what it feels like to lose a spouse. I lost my mother, younger brother, and two children, but to be a newlywed and to lose my husband. . . Well, I don't know the pain that you've endured because of that. But Mason does. You should talk with him, Katie. He can help you."

Her aunt squeezed Katie's shoulders. "I can only love you and encourage you to talk to God. He knows your pain and can help you through—if you'll let Him."

Katie gave her aunt a weak smile. "I hadn't thought to talk to Uncle Mason. Actually, I've avoided it because I knew he'd tell me I shouldn't be angry at God."

"Having lost his wife when he was young, he knows what

you're feeling. He was mad at God, too—ready to turn you and Jimmy over to your unscrupulous father. Then he was heading west, planning to leave behind everyone he ever loved."

Katie nodded, remembering the story of how he had lost his pregnant wife and his sister—Katie and Jimmy's mother—in a wagon accident. Why hadn't she realized before that he would understand what she was feeling?

She folded up the blanket and laid it back in the trunk. Tonight, if he had time, she'd talk with her uncle.

"You've been fussing about wanting something to do." Rebekah glanced at Katie with an ornery twinkle in her eye. "I thought maybe you'd want to get started mending these diapers. Some of them need to be rehemmed. You're welcome to use whatever you want in here."

Katie hugged her aunt, inhaling her faint scent of lavender mixed with the aroma of the cooked food. "Thank you. This is just what I need to keep me busy for a while."

"If you find it difficult to sew with that cast on, I'm sure Deborah wouldn't mind helping you." Rebekah handed Katie a little basket with various colored threads, a couple of needles, and a pair of scissors. "I need to check on that apple pie I have baking."

Katie sorted through the diapers and took out the ones that needed mending; then she took them and the basket into the parlor and sat down in the chair by a large window. She preferred to sit on the porch, but cold weather had blown in several days earlier; now it was simply too chilly.

Half an hour later, she heard steps on the front porch and glanced out the window. Her heart skipped a beat, and she pricked her finger with the needle when she saw Dusty

McIntyre. Katie wiped off the dot of blood, wrapped a scrap of cloth around her finger, and went to the door. Just about the time she got Dusty McIntyre out of her system, he showed up again.

He held a large package wrapped in brown paper and tied with twine in one arm and yanked his hat off with his other hand. "Afternoon."

Katie didn't want to think how intriguing he looked with his hair messed up like that and a shy grin on his nicely formed lips. His long duster hung open, and a deputy's badge pinned to his vest gave him an air of authority. Having seen him in action, Katie knew she wouldn't want to be on his bad side.

Realizing she was staring, she moved back. "C'mon in."

He stepped inside, hung his hat on a peg, and shrugged out of his duster and draped it on a hook—just as if he belonged there. He smelled of horse and leather and the faint hint of some kind of aftershave.

"Did you come to see Uncle Mason?"

Dusty shook his head and grinned, sending her heart into spasms.

"Seems we have this conversation every time I show up. I came to see you."

Katie didn't want to consider that she was actually glad he'd come to see her. She motioned him into the parlor and closed the front door.

Rebekah peeked out of the kitchen. "We got company?"

"It's just Dusty. He came to see me."

Her aunt's eyebrows lifted, and an ornery grin tugged at her lips. "Oh, I see. It's chilly out. I'll just fix you two some hot tea."

"I imagine he'd prefer coffee." Katie darted a glance at Dusty, and he nodded his head.

"Coffee it is." Rebekah disappeared back into the kitchen.

Katie ambled into the parlor, wondering how she knew Dusty wanted coffee instead of tea. Perhaps it was just that manly look of his that made her think he was a coffee drinker.

She motioned to Dusty to sit down and took a seat across from him. His long form looked awkward in the small side chair. "So, what brings you here today?"

Dusty glanced at the package in his lap. "I. . .uh. . .got to thinking about what you said about wanting to ask the dressmaker for some work. Trust me, I understand your desire for independence."

Katie watched him, wondering where this was leading. Seeing a tough lawman blushing was rather enchanting.

"Well, the truth is, I need some new shirts, and I can't find store-bought ones that fit since I have long arms. I got some cloth and was hoping I could hire you to make a couple."

Katie stared at him, stunned by the thoughtfulness of his offer. He wouldn't take her to town, but he brought some business to her. "I. . .well, sure! I'd be happy to. Show me what you've got in your package." She couldn't help grinning.

He untied the twine, and the paper crackled as it fell open to reveal a soft blue denim and a stark white cotton fabric. Katie crossed the room and fingered the cloth.

"This should do nicely." On top of the fabric lay a colorful tin box. "What's in that?"

Dusty's bronze cheeks took on a dark rosy shade. "I told Mrs. Whitaker at the mercantile how you lost everything in the fire, and she gathered some sewing tools she thought you would need. Consider it a gift from me for all the trouble I caused you."

She blinked. Who was this man? Why was he treating her so kindly after she'd been so mean to him? Guilt washed over her, making her realize how rude and unmannerly she'd been. She swallowed the lump in her throat and fought the tears in her eyes. Turning away, she stared out the window to gather her composure.

The settee squeaked as Dusty rose. She could feel him standing behind her.

"I'm sorry if I upset you. It wasn't my intent."

Katie closed her eyes. The concern in his voice was for her. Never once did Allan voice apprehension on her part. How could she have been so blind about him?

With her emotions once again under control, she turned to face Dusty. She owed him the truth. "You didn't upset me. I was just moved by your thoughtfulness."

Relief softened his gaze. Katie eased around him, her insides quivering like warm custard at being so close to him.

"Let's just see what's in that box. I'll need to measure you if I'm going to make those shirts." She pulled off the lid, and excitement coursed through her. The box held a shiny new pair of scissors, threads of all colors, a whole package of needles, a thimble, buttons, and a measuring tape. "Oh my, this is wonderful! But it's too much." She turned around. "You must let me make one shirt to pay you back for all these supplies."

Dusty shook his head. "No, they're a gift. I'll pay for the shirts."

"But—"

He held up his big, callused hand. "No buts. Or I'll take my business elsewhere."

Dishes clinked as Rebekah entered the room. "It's a pleasure to see you again, Mr. McIntyre."

"Look what he brought." Katie held out the tin box. "I'm going to make him some shirts."

Rebekah set the tray of coffee and cookies on the round table in front of the window. "How nice. That will keep you busy and out of my hair for a while." She smiled. "Well, I'll let you get back to your business."

"Thank you." Dusty nodded at Rebekah on her way out of the parlor.

"Let me measure you; then we'll take refreshment."

"All right."

Katie stretched the tape along Dusty's arms, noticing that he was correct in his assessment. He did have longer arms than an average man. She stood in front of him, trying to figure out how to best measure around him. "Hold up your arms so I can size your chest."

He did as he was told, but his cheeks looked a tad more flushed than normal. Katie held one end of the tape measure in the hand with the cast and leaned forward, running the tape behind Dusty's back. For a split second her cheek rested against his chest, and she could hear the steady beat of his heart. Her hands shook, and her mouth went dry. She noted the size, quickly moved away, and jotted the numbers on a piece of paper. Stepping behind him, she measured his shoulders across the back and the length the shirt needed to be.

"So, how do you come by the name McIntyre? Isn't that Irish?" she asked, hoping he wouldn't notice her nervousness.

Dusty cleared his throat and lowered his arms. "My father came from Scotland years ago, and his family moved to Kansas. After a while, Dad got itchy feet and decided to travel south. He didn't get very far. Fell in love with the daughter of a Cherokee chief and married her."

Intrigued, Katie motioned him to sit; then she served the coffee. "So you're half Cherokee. That explains your coloring."

Dusty nodded and sipped his coffee. "I wondered if your uncle might have Indian blood."

Katie sat down and shook her head. "I don't believe so. I've always heard he's part French."

He shrugged. "I just wondered."

Katie picked up the fabric. "So you want a shirt from the denim and the white cotton, but what about this?" She held up a soft, light blue flannel. "A nightshirt, perhaps?"

Dusty eye's widened, and he looked as if he'd choked on his cookie. "No! That's for the baby." If his cheeks hadn't been red before, they sure were now.

Katie bit back a grin at his embarrassment, then realized what he said. "I can't accept another gift from you, no matter how kind it is. It simply wouldn't be proper."

This time Dusty grinned, making cornmeal mush of her emotions. "I didn't say it was for you. It's for the baby. And I can give the baby a gift if I want to."

Katie studied the man before her. She'd been so wrong about him.

eight

A week later, Dusty rode up to the Danfield barn and reined Shadow to a halt. The front door of the house banged, and the saddle creaked as he twisted toward the noise. Nathan jumped off the porch, ignoring the steps, and Nick followed.

"I'm gonna git you, ya mangy outlaw," Nick yelled at his brother.

"Nuh-uh. I'm Jesse James, and you can't catch me." Nathan dodged around the water trough, then made a wide arc around Shadow's hind end.

Dusty tightened the reins. Shadow was a steady mount but not used to noisy little boys.

Nathan smiled and waved as he ran by. "Howdy, Dusty."

"Ma said to call him Mr. McAtire," Nick countered as he and his brother plowed to a stop beside Shadow.

Dusty bit back a smile at the mispronunciation of his name. He dismounted and held the reins loose while Shadow drank from the trough.

"Well, I cain't say that." Nathan blew out a breath that lifted his straight bangs in the air.

"You boys reckon you could tend to my horse in exchange for a peppermint stick?"

The twins' eyes widened, and they nodded. "Boy, howdy!"

Dusty smiled. How did they always manage to reply in the same way at exactly the same time? "No more water for him, though. At least not for a while."

"We know." Nathan held out his hand.

Dusty laid the reins across the boy's little palm. He pulled the sack of candy from his pocket and handed two red-and-white-striped sticks to Nick. "You be in charge of these since Nathan has Shadow."

Nick nodded and licked his lips as his hand closed around the candy.

Mason moseyed out of the barn and smiled when he saw Dusty. "You boys can put that horse in the third stall. And don't overfeed him." He lifted his hand in greeting. "Howdy."

Dusty closed the distance between them and shook Mason's hand. "Afternoon."

Mason eyed him until Dusty squirmed. What was he looking at?

"I halfway expected to see you two days ago."

Dusty blinked, wondering if he'd missed an appointment. "The marshal had me escort a forger he had in jail up to Tulsa. I just got back last night. Why were you expecting me?"

"You mean you don't know?"

Dusty searched his mind but had no idea what Mason was talking about. He shook his head.

Mason's whole face lit up like a child peeking in his Christmas stocking. "Katie had the baby. I guess Marshal White forgot to tell you."

All manner of emotions swarmed Dusty at the same time. This baby was alive because he had rescued Katie. On the other hand, the child would have been born in its own home if not for the fire caused by Dusty's charging in and capturing Sloane. At least the baby wouldn't be raised by a ruthless outlaw.

"It's an amazing thing when a child is born," Mason said,

probably misinterpreting his silence for awe.

"Yes, you're right. I probably should come back another day to give Katie time to rest up. I just wanted to see if she'd had a chance to sew up one of my shirts, but it sounds like she's been busy with other things."

"I believe she managed to get one done." Mason clapped him on the shoulder. "Let's go ask her. Maybe you can see the baby if he's awake."

Dusty walked beside Mason. "He?"

"Yep, she had a son. That's what she wanted—a son to carry on Jarrod's name."

"That's good. How's she doing?" Dusty hoped he wasn't crossing too many rules of propriety with his personal questions, but the Danfield family didn't seem too big on those rules.

"Great." Mason chuckled and glanced at Dusty with a twinkle in his dark eyes. "Nathan was disappointed to discover Katie had swallowed a baby instead of a pumpkin."

Dusty laughed, imaging the boy's confounded expression. He followed Mason into the house, where they shed their hats and coats, then meandered down the hall and into the kitchen. Rebekah and Deborah both looked up and smiled.

Rebekah wiped her hands on her apron and crossed the room. "Welcome, Mr. McIntyre. Come to see the baby?"

Dusty nodded. The fragrant scents and cozy atmosphere of the crowded kitchen made him long for a home of his own. For now, he was satisfied to live with the widower marshal and save money, but down the road, he'd like to get a little place of his own.

"Deborah, would you please tell Katie she has company?"

The young girl nodded, skirted around Dusty with a

whimsical grin tilting her lips, and disappeared into the hall. The kitchen door thudded open, and the twins charged in, both talking at once.

Rebekah grinned and looked at Dusty. "Why don't you wait in the parlor? It's much quieter there."

Dusty stood in the parlor a few minutes later, looking out a large window. South of the barn, he could see Josh chopping wood and could hear the dull thud as he tossed the split sections into a pile. Mason must have put the twins to work, because they were now stacking the chopped wood against the side of the barn.

Behind him, he heard footsteps and turned. A much slimmer version of Katie strolled in, followed by Deborah carrying the baby. Katie smiled, and his heart flip-flopped. She had never looked so beautiful. Her blue dress matched her eyes, but it was the glow emanating from her face that choked off his breath.

"It was so nice of you to come see us." Katie slowly eased down onto the settee, and Deborah handed her the baby, then quietly left the room.

Katie patted the cushion beside her. "Come sit beside me so you can hold Joey."

Dusty knew his eyes must have widened about as far as possible. He shook his head. "Uh. . .no, ma'am. I never held a baby before."

"Then it's time you know what it feels like. Come sit down, Dusty."

When she said his name like that, he could do nothing but obey. He dropped down beside her, trying to maintain a proper distance on the narrow settee. Katie unwound the blanket that enshrouded the baby. The infant squeaked, a tiny fist popped out, and the child stretched.

Dusty's heart pranced in his chest as he watched the little boy. This child's round face slightly resembled Katie's, and his fuzzy, blond hair reminded Dusty of a duckling.

She lifted the baby and handed him to Dusty. His hands trembled as he took the light bundle.

"This is Jarrod Joseph Hoffman Jr. But we call him Joey."

Her smile and the warmth in her eyes stirred something in Dusty that he hadn't felt in a long while. Worried that his big, rough hands would scratch the baby, he moved with caution.

"Support his neck with your left hand and his hind end with your right."

Dusty did as she suggested but held the baby away from his shirt. The child jumped and flung his arms out, nearly causing Dusty to drop him. He darted a gaze at Katie.

"Babies prefer to be held closely. Put Joey's head in the crook of your arm and cuddle him against your chest."

As Dusty tucked the baby against his shirt, he wondered again if he'd have been a father by now if Emily had lived. He studied Joey's cute, expressive face, and a deep longing for a family of his own enveloped him. Dusty thought he'd given up wanting a family, but in that second, he knew the truth. He wanted it all—a home, a wife, and children.

❧

Katie held her breath as Dusty hugged Joey to his chest. The longing in his eyes made her heart ache. She knew if she didn't get ahold of herself, she'd be in tears again. Aunt Rebekah said it was the natural way of things for a woman to cry a lot after a birthing.

She dashed to her feet, and Dusty looked up, bewildered. "I'll be right back. I need to get something."

If he hadn't looked so nervous, she might have laughed at his expression.

"You can't leave me here with—him. I wouldn't know what to do if he started crying."

Katie pressed her lips together at seeing this big, capable man floundering at holding a baby.

"Just jiggle him a little if he fusses. I'll be right back."

"No, Katie, wait—"

She rushed out of the parlor and slowly climbed the stairs to her bedroom, savoring her name on his tongue. She liked the sound of it way more than she should. In her room, she found the denim shirt she'd finished and pressed for Dusty and then made her way back downstairs.

As she entered the parlor, she heard Dusty talking and expected to see someone with him, but instead, she found him cooing softly to Joey. The baby stared at him with wide-eyed fascination.

For a fleeting second, a shiver of remorse coursed through her. Jarrod should be holding his child instead of this stranger. Katie closed her eyes and pushed away the angry thought. Nothing could change the past, and like it or not, Dusty had saved her life and Joey's. At the least, she owed him her kindness and gratitude. Putting her anger aside, she had to admit she was starting to like the quiet man. He reminded her of Uncle Mason.

He looked up, and relief flooded his eyes. "Good. You're back."

"Looks to me like you're doing just fine." Katie smiled and checked on her son. He wiggled as if he wanted Dusty's attention again.

"Well, what do you think?" She shook out the denim shirt

and looked at Dusty, wondering if he'd be pleased.

His eyes lit up, and she watched his gaze travel down the length of the sleeve. "That looks mighty fine. If you'll just take back your baby, I can get the coins I have in my pocket."

Katie grinned this time. He might enjoy holding the baby in private, but this tough deputy marshal didn't want to seem too soft in public. She folded the shirt and laid it on the coffee table, wishing she could ask Dusty to try it on but knowing that wouldn't be proper. She'd like to make sure the sleeves were long enough before she cut out the other one.

After settling back onto the settee, she reached out, and Dusty laid Joey in her arms. Katie tried to ignore the way her heart pitter-pattered when Dusty brushed against her arm.

He heaved a sigh that she was sure was relief. He stood and pulled two gold dollars from his pocket and set them on the table.

His boots thudded on the rag rug as he paced across the room. With his hands on his hips, he stared out the window. Disappointment surged through Katie. Did he dislike being near her that much?

Dusty stood tall and straight. Wide shoulders angled down to a narrow waist and long legs. His straight, dark hair hung past his collar in an appealing manner. Where Jarrod had been solid and stocky, Dusty was long and lean. She couldn't help being curious about him. And curiosity had gotten her into more trouble as a child than any of her other traits. She was tired of wondering why he was tracking Ed Sloane—or if he had a wife somewhere—or why he kept coming to see her.

"So, Dusty, do you have a family somewhere waiting on your return?"

Dusty's back stiffened, and he remained quiet so long

she thought he wasn't going to answer. Finally he shook his head. "No."

She barely heard his soft whisper. Determined to plod through the rock-hard soil of Dusty's past, she considered her next question. "You told me you spent a year and a half hunting down Al—I mean, Ed Sloane. Can I ask why? It just seems to me most lawmen would have given up a long time ago.

Dusty spun around, his mouth puckered and eyes blazing. "Not if that man had burnt down your home and killed your wife." His fists clenched so tight that his knuckles paled. He glanced down at Joey, and his expression quickly relaxed.

Confusion and pain muddled Katie's thoughts. It was true then. Ed Sloane really was a murderer. Dusty had saved her from making the worst mistake of her life. Losing her home was a small price to pay.

As she considered Dusty's words, surprise shot through Katie at the similarity of their experiences. She had been so wrong when she said he didn't know what she was feeling. Her angry statement that day must have hurt Dusty terribly. Compassion swirled through her, knowing he'd lost his spouse just as she had. "I'm so sorry. I didn't know."

He turned away and stared out the window again. "So now you can see that I do understand what you're going through and why I'm sorry for all the trouble I've caused you."

She wanted so much to go to his side, but with her hand still in the cast, she refused to carry Joey while she was walking. "Dusty, please look at me."

❧

Dusty was ready to bolt like a captured mustang that had broken its restraints. He wanted to walk out the door and ride off on Shadow, but he didn't want to be rude. He hated the pain of remembering. But as much as it hurt to talk about Emily and Sloane, in an odd way, it felt good. He turned to face Katie, and the sympathy in her gaze took his breath away.

"I'm so sorry for all the mean things I said to you." She looked away for a moment, then faced him. "People say things in anger when they are hurting. I blamed you for the fire—"

He winced at her words, knowing he was to blame for all her troubles.

"That was wrong. You weren't the one to knock over the lamp. You weren't even in the house when it happened."

He blinked, considering her words, and searched his mind, realizing she was telling the truth. There had been no lamp near the window that he dove through when he followed Sloane. He didn't start the fire. Sighing, he felt as if an anvil had been lifted off his chest.

"The truth is, I owe my life to you—and Joey's life." Katie stared up at him, sincerity blazing in her gaze. "And you kept me from making the horrible mistake of marrying—Ed Sloane."

She looked as if she could barely voice the words.

The remorse and condemnation he'd felt the past few weeks melted away. As he considered her words, he recognized the truth in them. He studied Katie as she watched her baby.

He admired her spirit and stubborn determination. She was lovely to look at with all that golden hair and her pretty eyes—even more so now that she was no longer tossing angry glares his way. She glanced up at him, making his heart skip.

"So, you see, you've helped me so much. I feel bad for the way I treated you. Will you please forgive me?"

Dusty didn't know how to respond. It was God's business to forgive, not his. But how could he resist those pleading eyes? He nodded, instantly rewarded with her glowing gaze.

Her bright smile broke down the walls of his heart, and he knew then that he cared more for her than he should.

He turned away again and stared out the window. "Thank you for making the shirt. It looks real nice." In truth, he couldn't imagine how she had managed to sew a whole shirt with her hand in a cast. That stubborn independence of hers was a driving force.

"You're quite welcome. After you get a chance to try it on, let me know how it fits. I'll wait to cut out the other one until I'm sure this one fits all right."

"Sure. That sounds sensible."

His heart soared, knowing he had a legitimate excuse to ride out and see Katie again, but he clamped down his emotions. He'd decided a long time ago that he didn't want to experience again the pain of losing someone he loved. He had to distance himself from Katie, yet he felt compelled to care for her.

Dusty hated these tugging emotions pulling him in two different directions.

The cast would surely come off in a few weeks. Until then, he'd maintain his distance and think up some other way to help Katie. But he wouldn't let his heart get any more involved. He'd help her until she was free of her cast. Then he'd ride off and try to forget about her.

nine

Dusty sat at the marshal's desk and studied the latest WANTED posters. It had been two weeks since he'd ridden out to the Danfield farm and seen Joey and retrieved his denim shirt. Looking down, he fingered the fabric and wondered if Katie had gone ahead and finished his other shirt even though he'd never told her how well the first one fit. He wanted to ride out and see her but knew he had to stay away if he was going to keep his heart intact.

The door creaked open, and a shadow darkened the doorway a moment before Mason walked in. Dusty smiled, happy to see the man again. He stood and held out his hand.

"Good to see you, Mason. What brings you to town?"

Mason solidly gripped his hand and smiled. "Jimmy's still down in Texas, and I needed some supplies."

Dusty waved his hand toward the empty chair in front of the window. He glanced outside, making sure things were quiet, then sat down in his chair.

Mason narrowed his eyes. "Why haven't you been out to the farm lately? Been busy?"

Dusty sighed, not wanting to talk about Katie and his feelings, but he couldn't lie. "No, things have been pretty quiet around here."

"Katie's missed you coming around."

Lifting his eyebrows, he looked at Mason, hoping he'd elaborate.

"She thinks maybe she scared you off because she asked about your past. Is that true?"

Mason's pointed question threw Dusty off guard. Though Mason was an honorable, God-fearing man, he didn't understand the depth of Dusty's pain. He didn't know how it felt to walk away from God and not be able to find your way back.

Mason stuck his feet out, crossed his ankles, and laced his fingers together behind his head, looking like he planned to stay for a while. "Let me tell you a story. I bet you didn't know that Rebekah is my second wife."

Dusty blinked, trying to imagine Mason married to someone else.

"A little over twenty years ago, I had a farm up St. Louis way. My sister and her husband owned the farm next to us. One day my wife and sister rode off in a wagon to help care for a sick neighbor. It started to rain while they were gone, and on the way home, they were crossing a low water bridge—" Mason closed his eyes as if remembering hurt him.

He looked at Dusty again. "They must have been in the middle of the river when a flash flood swept through. We found their bodies downstream near one of the dead horses. The wagon had broken apart, and most of it was gone."

Mason sat up and leaned forward. "Annie—my wife—was seven months pregnant with our first child."

Dusty's mouth went dry as he absorbed Mason's story. The man had experienced losing his wife, too. His pregnant wife. And his sister.

"Danielle, my sister, left behind two children—Jimmy and Katie. Jimmy was seven, and Katie only three. I buried the two women I loved most on this earth, sold my farm, and traveled to the Oklahoma Territory to find my brother-in-law, Jake. He was a low-life scoundrel who'd abandoned Danielle, preferring adventure over family."

Mason sighed and tightened his lips. "I was hurting so bad that I was determined to deliver Jimmy and Katie into his care, even though I'd been more a father to them than Jake ever had. Then I planned to head west and forget all those I'd ever loved."

"Wow, that's some story." Dusty ran his hand through his hair, feeling as if he should say something more comforting, but not knowing what.

"It's not a story. It's the truth. Jake talked me into riding in the Guthrie land rush. He got land, but I didn't. Afterwards, I was ready to leave town, though leaving the kids behind was about to do me in. Jimmy barely knew Jake, and Katie didn't remember him at all."

Dusty leaned forward with his elbows on the desk, engrossed in the tale. "So what happened? Obviously you didn't ride west."

"Jake approached me in the street. Said he wanted to talk to me. At the same time, an old man started hollering about how Jake had swindled him. The next thing I knew, Jake was shot and dying in my arms. Before he died, he pulled out the deed to his land and asked me to take care of the kids. After he died, I looked at the deed. Jake had put the land in my name instead of his."

"Whew! So what did you do?"

Mason settled back in his chair. "By then, I'd met Rebekah and fallen in love with her. But when I got back from the land run, I discovered she'd left town. I went after her. Rescued her from a couple of no-goods in Wichita, married her, and brought her back here. But before that, I had to let go of my anger. I was angry with Jake for abandoning his family. And mad at God for allowing Annie and Danielle to die. The pain was almost unbearable at first."

Dusty sat back, analyzing how similar their stories were. A spark of hope flamed to life. If Mason had found his way back to God, there must be hope for him, too. "How did you get past it all?"

"Falling in love with Rebekah helped. But I came to a point where I had to let go of my anger. Holding on to it was only hurting me—and nearly cost me the woman I was growing to love. I still don't know why God allowed what happened, but I would have never met Rebekah or had the family and life I have now if Annie hadn't died. We only see a speck of what's happening in our lives, but God sees the whole picture. I had to believe that He was watching my back. That's what you need to believe, too."

Dusty knew Mason was right, but how could he turn loose of his anger? It was what drove him to be who he was. And he couldn't get past the nagging question that haunted him: Why would God forgive a man who turned his back on Him just because life bucked him from the saddle?

Mason stood and stretched. "Well, don't be a stranger. We've all taken a liking to you. Come on out for dinner sometime and see how much Joey is growing. Katie would like to see you—oh, and she's got that other shirt ready. I offered to bring it to you, but she said no."

Mason grinned and moseyed out the door, not waiting for a response. The door clicked shut, and the sounds of the street faded. Dusty considered his words. He liked Mason and trusted him. But Mason had never hated anyone as much as

Dusty had Ed Sloane.

No, surely God wouldn't welcome him in His house, but maybe Katie would.

❧

"I can't believe how much Joey has grown since I last saw him."

Katie watched as Dusty held the baby against his chest. Her bright-eyed son made an O with his lips and stared up at him. Dusty put his finger against Joey's fingers, and the babe grasped it tightly.

He glanced wide-eyed at Katie. "Got quite a grip."

His smile tickled her belly. "Yes, but that's natural. All babies do that."

Rebekah walked in and set a tray of coffee and slices of cake on the table in front of the settee. "We're so glad to have you visit again, Mr. McIntyre."

Dusty peeked up at her. "Please call me Dusty."

Rebekah smiled. "All right then, Dusty. But you must call me Rebekah. Mason is finishing up in the barn and should be in soon. He'll be happy to see you again."

"I saw him when I rode in. Offered to help, but he said he and Josh could handle things."

"Well, I need to go help Deborah get the twins in bed. You and Katie go ahead and enjoy your cake and coffee. I'll be back in a little while."

Katie watched Dusty talk to her aunt. She enjoyed watching his lips and the way his mouth moved. When he looked down at Joey, his thick, dark lashes fanned his tanned cheeks, and his straight, coffee-colored hair hung down over his forehead. He'd often brush it back with his hand, but the straight strands seemed to have a mind of their own.

Dusty glanced up and caught her staring. Her heart

stampeded, but she couldn't look away. His gaze held hers, and she read the longing that she felt herself. Finally, she turned her head and stared at the sunset. Pinks and oranges wafted across the navy blue sky, silhouetting the barn in a dark shadow.

Now that she'd gotten over being angry with Dusty, she feared she was falling for him. How could she trust her heart after falling for the charms of an outlaw?

But Dusty was nothing like Ed Sloane. He was an honorable, law-upholding citizen.

Katie hated the confusion swarming in her mind. Was it possible to fall in love this quickly? Had she stayed angry with him so she wouldn't admit her true feelings?

Katie rose from her chair, pushing aside the unwanted thoughts. "You can lay Joey against the back of the settee so you can eat your cake. He doesn't turn over yet, so he'll be fine."

Dusty looked unsure but did as she suggested, making sure Joey was nestled safely against the back of the settee before he let go. His caution with her son made her value him more. If only she could trust her heart.

❧

Dusty savored the spicy apple cake as his eyes feasted on Katie. Her face had filled out a bit, and she didn't look as tired as she had right after having the baby. She took a small bite of cake and licked her lips, making him wish he had the right to pull her into his arms.

Would she accept his kisses?

She glanced up from her plate, checked on Joey, and then smiled at Dusty. He looked away, not wanting to think about what that smile did to his insides.

Why did he keep coming back here and torturing himself?

Even if he carried affections for Katie, nothing could come of it. He quickly finished his cake and swallowed down his coffee. It had been a mistake to come here.

She'd gotten over being angry with him, but the warm look in her eyes made him wonder if she was beginning to care for him. He couldn't continue to lead her on.

Nothing could come of their relationship other than friendship. He wouldn't allow it. To care for Katie meant he had to release his anger over Emily's death—and that wasn't something he was prepared to do.

Dusty stood, then realized he'd left Joey unsupervised and sat back down. Katie stared at him. "I should be heading out. It's nearly dark, and I've got a ways to ride."

Disappointment filled her eyes. "I suppose you're right. If you can sit there with Joey for a minute, I'll run upstairs and get your other shirt."

He nodded, and she flitted out of the room. Joey squeaked, so Dusty lifted up the baby and held him out in front of him. Making sure nobody was looking, he smacked his lips together. Joey turned his head and settled down, gazing intently at Dusty.

"You're some little fellow; you know it? Katie's mighty lucky to have you."

Moisture gathered in his eyes, and he blinked it away. He would have loved to have had a child, but if he had, he never would have tracked down and captured Sloane. And if ever there was a man who needed to be locked up in jail, it was he. Things were the way they were meant to be, and "what ifs" wouldn't change that.

Katie entered the parlor, holding his shirt up in front of her. "What do you think?"

He stood, cradling Joey in one arm, and nodded his approval of the finely constructed garment. Deborah followed Katie into the room and took the baby.

"I'll go change him for you, Katie. Good evening, Mr. McIntyre."

He watched Katie's cousin glide out of the parlor, taking Joey with her and leaving his arms empty. Dusty crossed the room, digging some coins from his pocket. He handed the money to Katie and held the shirt up between them. "Very nice. This will look good with my vest. Do you suppose you could make me another one?"

He lowered the shirt and saw Katie smiling at him. "Yes, I'd be happy to. I get my cast off next week, so it should be a lot easier and quicker."

Glancing at the cast, he wondered if it pained her to work on his shirts. "There's no rush. It can wait until you get the cast off."

"Well, I'll have to wait until you bring the fabric anyway."

He gazed into her eyes and watched the amusement die away as he stared at her. She didn't look away but licked her lips, making him want to yank her into his arms and kiss her until she forgot all about Ed Sloane and her late husband.

Her warm breath tickled his face, and he took a step closer. Kissing her would be a huge mistake, but it would be worth it. Her eyes widened as he leaned forward, but she didn't move away.

Dusty closed his eyes.

A loud thud sounded at the front door, making him jump. Katie moved back as the door banged open.

Josh ran past the parlor entrance, skidded to a halt, and dashed back. "It's Pa. He's hurt!"

ten

"Stay here," Dusty ordered Katie, as he charged out the door after Josh. He heard Katie sputter, but she didn't argue or follow him.

"What happened?" Dusty asked as he ran beside Josh.

"Loading bales—in the loft. Some fell—on Pa."

The frantic look in Josh's eyes told Dusty the boy was scared. They raced to the barn and through the open doors. Dust and stems of hay still sprinkled down from where Mason and Josh had been stacking bales in the loft.

Close to a dozen bales lay haphazardly in a pile, and somewhere, Mason was buried beneath them. The horses in their stalls nickered and stamped their hooves. Dusty grabbed the first bale and slung it aside, ignoring how the binder twine bit into his hands.

Josh tossed him a pair of gloves. Dusty slipped them on and yanked another bale off the pile. Behind him, he heard someone running in their direction. Josh tugged and heaved a bale to the side, revealing a boot. Dusty heard a gasp behind him and looked over his shoulder. Rebekah watched with one hand over her mouth, her eyes wide with concern.

Dusty flung aside another of the heavy bales. He moved around to where Mason's head should be and jerked off two more bundles. Rebekah set the lantern on a wooden crate and moved to Josh's side to help him.

Dusty heard a groan and pulled off another bale, revealing

Mason's head and shoulders. Mason coughed but didn't look up. Quickly, they removed the last few bales covering him.

Rebekah darted to his side and knelt in the hay. "Mason, honey, are you all right?"

Mason lifted his head, coughed, and grimaced.

Rebekah pulled little stems of hay from his dirty hair and brushed off his shoulders. "Tell me where you hurt."

"My side. Broken rib, maybe." Mason tried to push up but collapsed on the ground. "Got the wind knocked out."

"Can you move your legs?" Dusty hoped his friend wasn't seriously hurt, but he suspected Mason had more than one broken rib judging by the pain etched on his face.

Mason wiggled his feet, then moaned.

"We need to get him back to the house." Rebekah glanced up at Dusty. "Do you think you and Josh can carry him?"

"No, I can walk." Mason attempted to push up on his hands.

Dusty stooped and lifted Mason's arm over his shoulder, knowing it must pain him, but the act would allow Mason to keep his dignity in front of his family. Josh hurried to the other side, and they slowly made their way toward the house.

❧

"I can't thank you enough for staying at the farm and helping us while Uncle Mason mends." Katie lifted her head and peered out from beneath her sunbonnet, her sparkling blue eyes revealing her gratitude.

"I'm just glad things were quiet in town and Marshal White said he could do without me for a few days." Dusty clicked his tongue in his cheek and urged the team of horses to pick up their pace. The outline of Guthrie appeared on the horizon as they topped the hill.

For the past week he'd helped around the Danfield farm

while Mason recovered. Thankfully, Mason's ribs had only been bruised and not busted, but he did have a concussion. Rebekah's and Katie's hands had been full trying to keep the restless farmer in bed so he could heal properly.

Dusty had been thrilled when Rebekah suggested he take Katie to Guthrie for the big fall festival.

As they followed other wagons into town, excitement coursed through Dusty at spending the day with Katie at the big gathering. He glanced at Joey, sleeping quietly in Katie's lap. The baby sucked his thumb, and his eyelids moved as if he were dreaming.

Contented warmth oozed through Dusty. He had tried to fight his growing attraction to Katie, but being around her daily and eating meals with her made it nearly impossible. Dare he dream that she might one day return his affections? And was it being disloyal to Emily to hope Katie might?

Katie fidgeted on the seat beside him as he pulled the team under one of the last unoccupied trees. "I'm so excited. I've always loved coming to town for big celebrations like this."

Her excitement was infectious, and he couldn't help smiling. It had been a long time—years even—since he felt so lighthearted.

"Don't let me forget to buy flannel before we leave. I need to make some more diapers for Joey. It seems like I'm doing laundry every day."

"You want me to carry Joey for a while?"

Katie nodded and handed the baby to him; then he helped her alight from the wagon. "I'm so glad Doc cut off my cast when he came out to check on Uncle Mason. My wrist is still a bit stiff, so it's a challenge to manage Joey and my long skirt." She twisted her arm in front of him as if to prove her point.

The townsfolk cast curious stares in their direction as they walked down the boardwalk. Dusty could only imagine what they were thinking. Many had known Katie all her life, and most knew him from his job as deputy marshal. He ushered Katie toward the mercantile. "Ever had one of those new soda pops?"

"Oh yes!" Her eyes sparkled with delight. Katie loosened her bonnet and tugged it off. "Jarrod and I tried one in Claremont. It was delicious. And so bubbly."

Dusty peered out the corner of his eye at Katie. Mentioning her deceased husband hadn't seemed to dampen her enthusiasm. He breathed a sigh of relief. He didn't want anything to spoil this day.

After drinking a soda at the mercantile, they meandered around the booths and shops. The morning sped by as they watched the horse races and cheered on their favorite riders.

"Would you look at that!" Katie pointed at a trick roper and stared with her mouth open. "That's amazing."

The cowboy swung an eight-foot circle of lariat over his head. Then he lowered the loop and danced in and out of it, all the time keeping the rope spinning. Dusty nodded, impressed by the man's expertise, too.

Joey squirmed in Dusty's arms and started fussing. Katie studied the ground, a nice blush tinting her face. "I probably should change him and find somewhere to feed him."

Dusty could tell she was uncomfortable discussing the subject with him. "Let's go back to the wagon. It's shady there and probably about as quiet as any place in town."

Katie nodded and took his arm as he led her back to the wagon.

After fixing a blanket for Katie to rest on, Dusty moseyed

through town. He'd seen signs of a rifle shoot at the far end of Guthrie and made his way over there, stopping at the marshal's office long enough to pick up his favorite Winchester. He'd always been an expert marksman, and a shooting contest was just the thing to take his mind off Katie for a time.

❧

"I still can't believe you won that beautiful quilt in the rifle shoot. I've always admired Maude Wilson's handiwork. Her quilts are the loveliest ones around these parts." Katie glanced at the colorful coverlet lying in the back of the wagon, then smiled at Dusty. She couldn't believe he'd given her something so nice. She probably shouldn't accept the gift but didn't want to hurt his feelings, and she desperately wanted the lovely Flying Geese quilt. "Are you sure you don't want to keep it?"

"No, I want you to have it. Too fancy for me." Dusty shook the reins and clicked his tongue to keep the team moving.

Katie tried to ignore the way her shoulder bumped against Dusty's whenever the wagon traveled through a rut in the road. She glanced at Joey, who lay in her lap, looking around. He stuck a finger in his mouth and frowned, probably realizing it wasn't his thumb. Love for her son bubbled up inside her.

With the sun behind her, she shed her bonnet and tossed it in the back of the wagon, allowing the light breeze to cool her. Though she hated leaving town before the evening festivities, they needed to get home before dark. She'd had a wonderful time and gotten the flannel she needed. She'd hoped to chat with the dressmaker; however, the woman's shop was closed, and Katie never saw Miss Petit in town. At least Dusty had picked out material for two more shirts.

Katie peeked sideways at him, noticing the pleasing way he filled out the denim shirt she'd made him. A shadow of dark stubble shaded his cheeks, and his hair hung just past his collar, giving him a wild, untamed look. No wonder the single women in town kept casting him shy glances. Dusty was a fine-looking man.

He'd spent the day with her, even though he could have his choice of women. That thought sent a shiver of delight surging through her.

Katie hid a yawn behind her hand. She'd had a nice time, but it was a long day for a woman who'd recently had a baby. She wanted to lay her head on Dusty's shoulder but resisted the temptation. Riding home like this felt almost as if they were a family returning from a pleasant day in town.

Dusty laid the reins across his leg, lifted his hat, and rubbed his brow. He looked sideways and caught her staring. His gaze held hers, and she couldn't look away. She stared into his searing black eyes, her heart stampeding.

Joey let out a squeal, and she broke the connection and glanced at her son.

What had just happened?

She lifted Joey onto her left shoulder, creating a barrier between her and Dusty.

Did Dusty feel what she did? And just exactly what did she feel?

Once she'd gotten over being angry with him, she realized what a kind, considerate man he was. She knew he only kept coming around because of his guilt over the fire and her injury, but she wished that he harbored an attraction to her like she felt for him.

Yet Dusty still loved his first wife. She could tell from the things he'd said to her. He held on to his anger over Emily's tragic death, just as she'd clung to her anger about the fire and her ruined wedding. But she'd been wrong to do so, and he needed to see that it was bad for him. Holding on to anger only hurt the one doing the holding. It had turned her into a grumpy, bitter person. But no more.

That night, after they returned to the farm and Joey had nursed and was asleep, Katie knelt down beside her bed.

"Father God, forgive me for all the anger I've harbored against Dusty. I know now that he was only doing his job and that he saved me from marrying an outlaw and making a horrible mistake. I was angry about the fire and losing my possessions, but You saved my life and my sweet son's. Thank You, Father. And please help Dusty to turn loose of his anger and make peace with You."

&

"That Deputy McIntyre is a mighty handsome man." Emmylou Tompkins batted her eyelashes in Dusty's direction. "You're fortunate to be keeping his company."

Katie watched Dusty darting back and forth, trying to corral the twins. They'd brought the children to church so that Mason and Rebekah could enjoy the morning alone. Uncle Mason was finally getting around again, but he couldn't do much yet. Aunt Rebekah feared the jarring of the wagon would set him back, so they'd stayed home from church.

Katie looked at Emmylou. "I'm not keeping company with Mr. McIntyre. He's helping out on the farm because my uncle got injured."

Emmylou flounced beside Katie. "Well, that's just my point. Why him? Why is the deputy marshal doing menial labor on your farm?"

Katie sighed. "It's a long story, and I don't want to get into it now."

Emmylou's lips puckered and twisted to one side. "Well, any of the unmarried women in town would gladly trade places with you."

The nosy woman didn't like being kept in the dark. Katie could only imagine what Emmylou would do if she knew that Katie had nearly married an outlaw. She tightened her lips to keep from giggling at the aghast expression that surely would have been on the woman's face.

Dusty strode toward her with a squirming, giggling twin under each arm. "Got these two hooligans corralled. Did you find Deborah?"

Katie peered across the churchyard to where her cousin stood holding Joey, surrounded by a group of chattering girls. Josh stood off to the side with two friends, feigning lack of interest, at the same time covertly watching the group of females. Katie sighed. Her cousins were growing up.

Dusty deposited the twins in the back of the wagon. "Now stay put until we get underway. I don't want to have to go hunting you down again."

Both wide-eyed boys sat down and stared at him. Katie wondered if they were surprised at this sterner version of Dusty. He'd used his lawman's voice to get the spirited boys under control, and it seemed to be working.

Katie allowed him to help her onto the wagon seat. She tied her bonnet strings under her chin and adjusted her skirts, ready to get home and out of the warmth of the Indian summer that had settled over the land. The wagon tilted and creaked as Dusty climbed up beside her. He let out a shrill whistle that made both her and the horses jump.

She gave him a questioning stare, and he grinned, sending her heart into spasms. He nodded his head toward the girls, and Katie saw that Deborah was walking toward them. "Civilized folk would simply walk over and tell Deborah it was time to leave."

He pushed back his western hat and looked at her, nudging his shoulder into hers. An ornery glint flashed in his eyes. "Who ever told you I was civilized?"

A delicious shiver snaked down Katie's spine. Dusty might like to believe he was as wild as a mustang, but she knew better. The man had a heart of gold, even if he'd never admit it.

Deborah handed Joey up to Dusty, who passed the baby to Katie. She cuddled her son and watched the clusters of church members break up and head for their wagons. Deborah climbed into the back of the wagon with Josh's assistance.

"I want to ride with Josh," Nick shouted.

"Nuh-uh. I want to." Nathan bounced to his feet and started to climb over the side.

Dusty turned around and stared at the boys, and they both sat back down. It amazed Katie how he could command the mischievous boys' obedience without even a word, when they'd barely listen to her and she'd known them all their lives.

"I don't mind if they take turns riding with me." Josh pulled his mare to a stop beside Dusty. "That is, if it's all right with you."

Dusty nodded. "Pick a number between one and twenty."

"Five." Nick jumped to his feet again.

"Ten." Nathan looked hopefully at Dusty.

"Nate wins. The number was twelve."

"Aw, no fair." Nick flopped down and crossed his arms.

"Nicholas David Danfield." Katie shot him a stern glare for his unruly response.

He ducked his head. "Sorry."

Nathan climbed on behind Josh and beamed his victory until Katie also gave him a look. Deborah pulled Nick against her side and started telling him a story as Dusty clucked to the horses.

"What did you think of the sermon?" Katie peered sideways at him.

"Good." He stared ahead, guiding the team around the McPherson and Robinson families, who stood beside the road, visiting. The women smiled and waved as they passed by. Dusty touched the brim of his hat.

Katie waved and smiled back. "Just good. That's all you have to say?"

"It's been a long time since I've been to church, and it felt good."

Katie stared at the dried prairie grass swaying in the warm breeze as the wagon rocked back and forth down the dirt road. Dusty's comment made her realize how little she really knew about him.

She couldn't deny her feelings had taken an unexpected turn. At some point, she'd grown to care for him. He was so kind it was hard not to care.

But she couldn't expect Dusty to hang around forever. One of these days, he would feel that he'd done enough penance and move on.

What would she do then?

She'd miss him, for sure.

She shouldn't be pondering on Dusty, but rather on how she was going to become independent again. She couldn't live with her aunt and uncle forever, no matter how loving and gracious they were. But how could a woman with a young child find work?

And what should she do about her feelings for Dusty?

eleven

Katie crossed the small bedroom, jiggling Joey on her shoulder. The baby cried and cried. Aunt Rebekah thought he was colicky or possibly teething, though he was still a bit young for that. Katie had tried to nurse him, but Joey pushed away and fussed. He wasn't one to refuse a meal, so her concern mounted. She even tried rubbing his stomach, but that didn't work.

She cooed to her son, aching for him. After another ten minutes of Katie walking and humming church hymns to him, Joey finally drifted off into a restless sleep. Her arms and back ached from standing and holding him so long. Did she dare try to lay him down?

When her arms and shoulders burned so much she was afraid she might drop her son, she carefully eased him into his cradle and covered him with a small quilt. Breathing a sigh of relief, she tiptoed out of the room and into the upstairs hallway.

"Yahoo! I'm gonna get ya, you mangy outlaw." Nathan barreled up the stairs, feet pounding on the wooden slats, right behind his brother, whose face was covered with a bandanna.

"You ain't catching me." Nick shouted over his shoulder. He dodged past Katie, and she grabbed his arm, then got ahold of Nathan.

"Hush!" she squealed in a loud whisper. "I just got Joey to

sleep. And you know your mom doesn't want you running in the house."

"But I'm an outlaw, and I gotta get away." Nick shrugged out of her grasp and charged for the stairs.

"Let me go, Katie. I gotta catch that mangy varmint." Nathan twisted and squirmed, then pulled free, racing after his brother.

Katie held her breath, hoping and praying their ruckus didn't wake Joey. When he didn't cry, she tiptoed to the stairs. As her foot hit the first step, Joey squeaked. Katie closed her eyes and uttered a quick prayer for strength for herself and peace for her son. How did a new mother ever get anything done?

As Joey's crying intensified, she turned around and went back into the bedroom. Maybe if she took him outside, he might quiet down. Carrying her son, Katie reentered the hallway but found Deborah blocking her path.

"Sorry, I was looking for the book I've been reading. Mom doesn't need me for a while, so I thought I'd read a chapter or two."

Katie stepped to her left at the same time Deborah did. She moved to the right side of the hall as her cousin did the same.

Deborah giggled. "Pa keeps saying this house is too small, and I think he's right. It wasn't so bad when you and Jimmy were gone, but it's crowded now that you're both home."

Katie knew Deborah was just stating the obvious, but her cousin's words cut her to the quick. Deb was right. Both Jimmy and Katie were grown adults and should be out on their own. She couldn't fault her brother though. After getting wounded in the Spanish-American War, he'd come home to recuperate. Now that he was well, he couldn't seem to find a place to settle. He would stay here a few months and then just ride off without anyone knowing where he'd gone.

She hated that he was so restless and missed him terribly when he was gone, but she knew war changed people—and it had changed her brother.

With the flannel blanket secure around Joey, she had a driving ache to find Jimmy. He'd returned two days ago but had been so busy she hadn't had time to have a good chat with him.

She looked in the kitchen and found it empty, then peeked in Rebekah and Mason's bedroom and found her aunt sitting in her chair in the corner of the room, sound asleep with a book on her chest. Katie hurried away lest Joey fuss and wake her.

Outside, she saw the boys running around the barn. One would think they'd need a nap by the hectic pace they kept, but Rebekah had given up when they turned four. It became such a battle to keep the active boys in their beds for a half-hour rest that she and Rebekah needed an hour-long nap to recover. At least the boys collapsed at night once in bed.

The barn door was open, so Katie wandered in, hoping to find Jimmy. She heard someone moving around in the loft and glanced up. "Who's up there?"

Jimmy peered down and smiled. "Hey, sis. Whatcha doing?"

"Walking Joey. He has been fussing all afternoon. How about you?"

"I'm just rearranging these hay bales so we can get some more up here."

"Can you take a break and talk to me for a few minutes?"

Jimmy swiped his arm across his forehead. "Sure. I could use a few minutes' rest." He grabbed a rope hanging from the ceiling and shinnied down. "What's wrong with my nephew?

I could hear him crying clear out here."

Katie sighed. "I wish I knew." She looked at Joey and realized he'd fallen back asleep.

"Let's sit on the porch." Jimmy's boots thudded on the hard dirt floor as he walked out of the barn.

"Where are Uncle Mason and Josh?" Katie asked.

Jimmy stopped at the well and took a swig of water from the bucket. "They're out in the field, loading more hay in the wagon."

"Should Uncle Mason be doing such difficult work so soon after his accident?"

Jimmy shrugged. "I offered to do it, but you know how stubborn he is. Rebekah should be glad he rested up a whole week. That's nothing short of a miracle."

"Just goes to show you how badly he was hurt. Plus Dusty was here to help out until you got back."

Jimmy lowered himself in the porch rocker, dusted off his shirt, and reached for Joey. Katie eyed his shirt and dirty hands.

"Aw, c'mon, sis. It's just hay. I promise I haven't shoveled any manure today."

Katie winced, then laid her son in her brother's arms. Jimmy loved kids and would make a great dad someday. If only he got over his wanderlust.

"Are you planning to stay long?" She sat in the rocker next to him and watched Jimmy's face.

He looked at Joey with a hunger that surprised her. Then he gazed off into the distance. She followed his stare and saw the twins galloping in the field toward their father. She felt a pang of regret that she wasn't watching them better, but then nobody could keep up with those two.

"I'm not sure how long I'll stay. I probably ought to be finding a place of my own before too long."

"You could always come live with me."

Jimmy looked at her, a lopsided grin pulling at one cheek. "I am living with you."

"Oh, you know what I mean." She smacked him on his arm.

"I'm guessing you mean your farm. Last I heard, you didn't have a house to live in."

"Maybe you could rebuild it?"

Jimmy pressed his lips together and stared at Joey. "I don't know, sis. I've heard there's talk of an oil strike up near Tulsa. I've been thinking of heading up there and seeing if I can find work."

"Tulsa! But that's at least two days' ride."

"Not by train."

"Well, no, but who has the money for a train? I sure don't." Katie hiked her chin, hurt that her brother wanted to leave again.

Jimmy laid his head back and closed his eyes.

She had no right to stop him if he wanted to go to Tulsa. And as much as she loved her family, she'd leave, too, if she had a choice. An eighteen-year-old woman had no business mooching off her relatives. And as crowded as her aunt and uncle's home was, she knew it would be a blessing to her family if she weren't there.

But where could she go?

If only Dusty returned her affections. Maybe they could—no. She'd come close once to marrying a man she'd only known a few months, and here she was toying with the idea of marrying a man she'd known only a few weeks. Was she daft?

But wasn't this different? God had brought Dusty into her life. Then again, hadn't she thought the same thing about Allan?

Katie sighed and leaned her head back against the rocker. Life was so complicated at times. How could her feelings for Dusty have grown so quickly? A few weeks ago, she despised him, but now he claimed a chunk of her heart. If she moved away, she'd never see him again, and that thought hurt as much as had losing her farmhouse to the fire. But she couldn't live with her aunt and uncle forever.

She looked toward the cloudy gray sky—a sky that mirrored her emotions. *What do I do, Lord? Show me the way You want me to go.*

&

Katie stood in line to exit the church building, the children behind her nudging her in the back and side in their anxiousness to get out and see their friends. "Hold your horses," she murmured.

Uncle Mason shook the parson's hand. "Mighty fine message today."

Parson Davis smiled. "Thank you, Mason. It's good to have you with us again."

"Good to be here."

After Rebekah and Josh greeted the minister, Katie stuck her fingers out from under Joey's blanket and shook the parson's hand. "Thank you for your message, sir."

He nodded and looked past her to the next person. Katie slipped outside, and the twins and Deborah dashed around her and down the porch steps. She found Rebekah talking with some of her friends. Joey was getting hungry, but there was no place in this crowd where she could feed him. Glancing around, her heart jumped when she saw Mrs. Howard, her teacher for her first few years of school.

The middle-aged woman caught her gaze and waved. "Katie dear, how are you?"

Katie smiled as the woman drew closer. "Fine. Thank you. How about you?"

Mrs. Howard pressed her lips together. "I'm doing well, though I miss Albert something awful."

"I know just what you mean."

"Oh, Katie, I'm sorry. How could I be so insensitive?" She laid her hand on Katie's arm and tilted her head. "I'd forgotten you also lost your husband. At least I had Albert for a good ten years. But let's not talk about sad things. Who's this sweet little fellow?"

Katie beamed a smile. "My son—Jarrod Joseph Hoffman Jr. But we call him Joey."

"My, my, but that name is a mouthful." She leaned over and touched Joey's head. "What a little darling. Albert and I were never blessed with children."

Katie winced. At least God had blessed her with a son. She empathized with Mrs. Howard and thought how lonely she must be.

"I'm teaching again—up in Cushing."

"Oh, that's wonderful. You always were my favorite teacher. I hated it when you left, even though I was happy that you got married."

"I missed all you children, too." Mrs. Howard pushed her wire-framed glasses up on her thin nose. "I thought you'd moved away. Are you living back in Guthrie again?"

"For a time. I have a farm near Claremont, but my house burned down, so I'm staying at Uncle Mason's for now. But

I hope to find a place of my own soon."

"Oh, you poor dear. You've been through so much for someone so young." She rested her elbow in her hand and tapped the forefinger of her other hand against her lips. "You know, I've been thinking about taking in a boarder or two. Would you possibly be interested in coming to live with me?"

Katie gasped. Could this be God's answer to her prayer?

Her first thought was that she'd probably never see Dusty again. But then wouldn't that be the best thing since he'd never care for her like she did him?

And he hadn't been at church today. This must be God's confirmation and provision.

"You know, Mrs. Howard, I just might take you up on your offer. That is, if you wouldn't mind a boarder with a child."

A smile broke out on the woman's face. "I'd be delighted!" She pulled a piece of paper from her handbag, fished out the stub of a pencil, and wrote something down. "Here's my address. I'll be in town for several more days, visiting my sister, Ida Johnson. Think about it and let me know before I leave town, if you can. But right now, I believe the marshal's deputy would like to speak with you." Her twinkling gaze focused on something past Katie's shoulder. "I'll look forward to hearing from you." She squeezed Katie's hand, then walked off to join her sister.

Katie whirled around, and her heart leaped at the sight of Dusty. He wore the white shirt she'd made him, although it wasn't too white at the moment. His black pants and vest were covered with dust, and Dusty stood twisting his sweat-stained hat in his hands. He looked as if he was trying to live up to his name. He must have just gotten home from a long, hard ride.

"You're moving away?"

The distressed expression on his face took her breath away, making her sorry that he'd overheard her conversation. Maybe he did care for her after all.

≥⦁

Dusty felt as though a horse had kicked him in the chest.

Katie was leaving.

Just when he realized that he cared deeply for her.

Katie blinked. "Well, it's not for sure yet, but yes, I'm thinking about moving in with Mrs. Howard, who lives in Cushing."

Dusty studied the ground and stood with his hands on his hips, knowing it was the only way he could keep them from trembling. How could he let her go? He'd lost the first woman he loved, although he couldn't help that, but this time, maybe he had a chance. He looked up and noted they were surrounded by people. All around him he could hear the chatter of small groups of townsfolk, squealing children at play, and laughter. What he needed to say couldn't be said here. "Will you walk with me for a bit?"

Katie nodded. She glanced around, found Deborah, and then motioned for the girl. "Would you mind watching Joey for a few minutes?"

Deborah's eyes lit up. "Of course not. My friends all love him." She carried off the baby and was quickly surrounded by a throng of adolescent girls.

Katie slipped her arm through Dusty's, and her hand felt warm against his solid arm. He guided her past the church and away from staring eyes.

While he was off chasing some cattle rustlers the past few days, he had considered his options. Now that Katie's cast was off, she no longer needed him to be responsible for her. The problem was he liked caring for her.

He'd thought things through, over and over again. There was only one answer. If Katie were to marry him, she'd have a husband to care and provide for her, and Joey would have a father. She could live in Guthrie and still be close to her family, but not dependent on them. If only she would agree.

He walked her past the parsonage, where the minister's wife had planted a multitude of chrysanthemums in front of her porch. Gold, dark red, and deep purple flowers brightened an otherwise-barren landscape. "Pretty, aren't they?"

Katie nodded, but Dusty thought she was prettier than any flower. She looked beautiful in that dark blue dress. Her hair was piled up onto the back of her head, with rebellious wisps that had escaped their binds curling around her face in an appealing manner.

He cleared his throat. "Listen, Katie, we don't have a lot of time before you'll need to go. I want to ask you something." Dusty's heart ricocheted in his chest as it did when he was closing in on a dangerous outlaw.

She stared at him wide-eyed, as if she expected him to say something strange. "What is it?"

"I don't want you to leave."

Katie blinked, and her brows dipped down. "Why not? You know how important my independence is to me."

Dusty crossed his arms, then uncrossed them and wiped his moist palms on his pants. He shoved his hands in his pocket. "Yeah, I know. That's why I've come up with a solution." He took a deep breath, then looked into her eyes. "I want you to marry me."

Katie opened her mouth, then closed it, staring at him as if he'd gone loco. "And just why should I consider such an idea?"

Dusty knew he wasn't much of a catch, but surely he hadn't been wrong in noticing the interest in Katie's eyes. "I. . .uh. . . have some money saved; we could get a little place of our own, and you wouldn't have to stay with your relations. It wouldn't be what you're used to, but you'd have a home again."

Katie's expression softened, and she looked off. "Is that the only reason? So I'd no longer have to mooch off my relatives?"

When she faced him again, anger smoldered in her gaze. "You don't have to take care of me forever. I appreciate your thoughtfulness, but you've done enough."

Dusty stood dumbfounded as she walked away. How had he managed to mess things up so thoroughly? She'd completely misunderstood him.

He jogged past her, blocking the way. His hands rested on her shoulders. Katie stopped and looked up at him. His chest clenched at the tears shimmering in her eyes. One tear escaped, and he wiped it away with his finger.

"Katie, I think you've misunderstood. I want to marry you because I care for you, not because I feel some obligation."

She blinked her eyes as if in disbelief. "You care for me? Truly?"

A slow smile tugged at his lips. "Yes, I do. Truly."

Katie swiped her tears with her hand and gazed up at him. "I've grown to care for you, too. A lot."

A joy unlike any he'd experienced in a long time surged through him. "So is that a yes?"

"Yes!" Her cry bubbled up on a laugh, and joy illuminated her countenance. "Yes, I'll marry you."

Stunned, Dusty stood there, unsure what to do next. He was getting married again. A slow ecstasy flooded through his body. He picked up Katie's hands and pressed a kiss on her knuckles.

She tugged a hand free and reached up, caressing his cheek. "I love you, Dusty."

He closed his eyes and savored the moment, then hauled her into his arms and kissed her. The warmth of her lips on his was the ultimate reward for all he'd been through. Walking away from a job he loved, leaving his hometown, and recklessly searching for Sloane—all had been worth it for Katie's kiss and hearing her say she loved him.

Behind them, someone cleared his throat. They jumped apart, breathless. By the red stain to her cheeks, Dusty could tell Katie was embarrassed, but then she looked past him; and all color drained from her face.

Dusty turned around, still breathing hard and his body trembling. His emotions skidded to a halt when he saw Mason standing there with his arms crossed over his chest, glaring at them.

twelve

Katie had done her best to avoid Uncle Mason's stare ever since arriving home from church. She busied herself in the kitchen, helping her quiet aunt get dinner on the table, then hid out in her room after the meal. Now that Joey had eaten and was sleeping, she sat in her rocker, making a list of things to do for the wedding.

Disappointment surged through her when she realized neither her aunt nor uncle was pleased with her decision to marry Dusty. How could they not approve when they both liked him so much?

Surely she wasn't making another mistake.

No, she couldn't be, not when she saw such affection in Dusty's eyes. He hadn't come right out and said he loved her, but he said he cared for her. And that kiss. . .*oh, my*!

If he cared as much as his kiss indicated, surely love would soon follow.

Katie touched her lips. Jarrod had never been much of a kisser. He hadn't expressed his affections well, though she never doubted his love. And Allan. . .*eww*! Just the thought of his urgent kisses gave her the shivers.

But Dusty's kiss—well, he made her quiver, too, but in a nice way.

She rested her hands in her lap and stared out the window. She had prayed and asked God to show her the way to go, and He'd given her two separate paths to choose from. Had she picked the correct one?

A soft knock sounded on her bedroom door, and it slowly opened. Aunt Rebekah peeked in and gave her a weak smile. "If you're not too tired, Mason and I would like to talk with you in the parlor."

Katie swallowed the lump in her throat. How many times in her life had she endured the "parlor talk"?

There was no sense in avoiding the inevitable, and she nodded. She checked on Joey, wishing with all her heart that he'd wake up and need her, but he slept soundly. For a brief moment she was tempted to give him a little pinch to make him cry, but she shook off that desperate thought.

In the parlor, she took a chair near the window. Rebekah sat on the settee, and Mason paced in front of the fireplace. Katie rubbed her finger back and forth on the wooden trim of the chair, took a steadying breath, and waited for her uncle to speak.

Finally, he looked at Rebekah, who nodded her head. He turned toward Katie. Her pulse kicked up a notch, and she felt like she had when she was eight years old and had nearly set the barn on fire because she'd decided her dolly was cold.

"Katie, you know your aunt and I love you dearly."

She nodded, knowing they couldn't have cared for her any more than if she were their own child.

"Rebekah and I have discussed it, and we both feel you're making a huge mistake. I haven't pushed you to talk about this other man you nearly married, but the fact that you didn't want to tell us about him leads me to think you sensed marrying him was the wrong thing. You tried to hide the news from us until it was too late to stop it. And now here you are, ready to marry another man you've known only a month or so."

Katie winced. Spelled out so clearly, she could understand why he'd be concerned.

Mason rubbed the back of his neck. "I think you know we both like and respect Dusty."

Katie tightened her grip on her skirt. "Then why do you disapprove of us marrying?"

Mason glanced at Rebekah as if he needed backup. She pressed her lips together and nodded. "For one, you seem to be rushing into this marriage."

Rebekah tugged a sofa pillow onto her lap. "Katie, you've always been one to make hasty decisions instead of taking the time to think things out and pray over the situation."

"But I did pray for God's guidance. And then Dusty asked me to marry him. Isn't that confirmation?"

"You're confusing confirmation with coincidence. They aren't the same thing." Rebekah heaved a sigh and looked out the window.

Katie heard the twins race by outside, followed by Josh, who yelled at them to slow down.

"The biggest issue is that Dusty isn't right with God. He's still angry over losing his first wife, and that's no way to start out a new marriage. Trust me, I know." Uncle Mason's gaze begged her to believe him.

"But he said he cares for me." She blinked back the tears stinging her eyes and burning her throat.

"I believe he does. Dusty is a man who takes responsibility very seriously, and he feels somewhat responsible for what happened to you." Mason lowered himself to sit by Rebekah. "But he has no business getting married to you when he's at odds with the Lord."

Suddenly, Katie felt the blood drain from her face. She'd

done it again. She had plowed ahead and agreed to marry a man without making sure he was walking with God.

How could she be so dumb?

"Are you all right, sweetie?" Aunt Rebekah's concerned tone nearly did her in.

Was she so desperate to not mooch off her relatives that she'd marry the first man who asked her? How could she be so naive?

She closed her eyes and muttered a prayer. She knew it in her heart now—she was wrong to accept Dusty's proposal. As a Christian, it would be a mistake to marry a man whose heart wasn't right with God, no matter how good that man was. The thought of hurting Dusty caused her stomach to clench with queasiness, but she had to put a halt to their marriage plans.

❧

"What do you mean Katie is gone?" Dusty leaped to his feet. The chair he was sitting in clanked against the wall. He stared at Mason, fighting the confusion and an unwanted numbness that made his whole body feel heavy and sluggish.

Mason twisted the brim of his hat. "She decided to move to Cushing and live with the widow Howard for a time."

Dusty ran his hand through his hair. "I don't understand. When I talked to her Sunday, she agreed to marry me."

Mason studied the floor for a few moments. Dusty knew from the look on his face when Mason had caught them kissing that he'd been upset. His fists tightened. Had Mason influenced Katie in leaving him?

"Mind if I sit down?" Mason motioned to the chair in front of the window.

Dusty nodded and grabbed his own chair, dropping into it, feeling as if he'd lost something precious.

"Katie has been through a lot lately. You know that more than any of us since you experienced some of it. On top of that, after women have a child, their emotions are all aflutter, and they can't seem to think clearly for a time. Trust me, I experienced it enough times with Rebekah."

Mason's ears turned red as he looked at Dusty, then at the floor again.

"I won't lie to you, Rebekah and I discouraged Katie from marrying you."

Dusty lunged to his feet again, feeling as if his friend had stabbed him in the back. "Why would you do that? You know I'd take good care of her and Joey. I care deeply for them both."

Mason grimaced, then nodded. "Yes, I know that, but the problem is, you're still angry at God for what happened to your first wife. You can't be the husband Katie needs until you make peace with Him."

Dusty stared at Mason. He clenched his jaw, biting back his angry retort. Katie was a grown woman who could make her own decisions. What right did Mason have to dissuade her from marrying him?

"Katie needs time to heal and to get her heart right with God. She's been dodging so many arrows sent her way that she hasn't had time to think things out. She's always been one to rush into things, then have to pay the consequences later." A gentle smile of remembrance tilted Mason's lips. "Did I ever tell you about the baby skunks she found?"

Dusty heaved a sigh and fell back into his chair, imagining what must have happened.

"She thought they were kittens." Mason glanced up. "They weren't, though, and Rebekah used nearly her whole store of tomatoes trying to get the stink off that little gal."

Dusty allowed a smile that didn't reach his heart. "Sounds like she had her share of trouble as a child."

"Yep, she did at that." Mason leaned forward, elbows on his knees and laced his fingers. "Katie will do the right thing in the end. If you and she are meant to be together, this time apart won't affect your relationship. In fact, it will make it stronger."

Dusty failed to understand that reasoning. He'd already lost Emily. He didn't know if his heart could stand losing Katie, too.

But what Mason had said about God made sense, even if he didn't want to admit it out loud. After Emily died, Dusty had plunged forward without thinking. He was afraid if he stopped to sort things out, he might just wither up and die from the pain of loss. Having Sloane to chase after gave him a target for his anger. But Sloane was in jail now, and Dusty needed to step back and turn loose of his hate.

His pride had taken a hit with Katie leaving town without explaining why she couldn't marry him or even saying good-bye.

"Dusty, I know what you're feeling." Mason looked at him with pleading eyes. "I lost my wife—not to a madman but to an act of nature. Something God could have easily prevented. I don't know why it happened, but I nearly let my anger and unforgiving spirit destroy my life."

He stood, crossing the small room to the desk, then placed his hands on the wood and leaned forward. Dusty wanted to back away from the intensity of his stare.

"You've got to put aside your anger, Dusty. Get right with God. Nothing in this world will make sense until you do.

And Katie can never be a part of your life if you don't."

Mason blew out a warm sigh that smelled of coffee and stood. He looked spent. For a man of few words, he'd sure spewed a lot today. Probably used up a whole fortnight's worth.

Mason settled his hat on his head. "I like you, Dusty. I consider you a friend, but you need to consider what I've said today. If you ever want to talk, you know where to find me."

The door clicked shut, and Dusty watched Mason stride by as he passed the window. Leaning his elbows on the desk, Dusty rested his head in his hands.

Katie was gone, and with her, his dream of starting over. He should have known better than to allow his emotions to get in the way.

He thought about the little house he'd just found and paid the first month's rent on. Now he wondered if he'd ever live there.

A restless energy zipped through him. He needed to get Shadow and ride out of town, shedding his pain as they soared across the prairie. He pulled open the drawer that held the WANTED posters and thumbed through them. Maybe he'd set out bounty hunting again. If he rode long enough and far enough, maybe he could outride his pain.

Mason's words came back to haunt him. *"You can't be the husband Katie needs until you make peace with Him."*

He rose and walked to the window. Pressing both hands to the glass, he stared outside. People ambled down the street, talking and laughing, oblivious to his struggle.

He'd felt God's gentle tugging, urging him to come back to the fold. He knew he should have sought God's forgiveness a long time ago, but he'd felt so unworthy. God didn't walk away from him; he left God. And what kind of a man runs away just because times get rough?

But Mason had done a similar thing—and he'd made peace with God. Perhaps Dusty could, too. God's arms were wide enough to wrap around a hardened warrior—if only that warrior would yield.

Dusty strode out of the office, slamming the door behind him and rattling the windows. It was past time he had a long talk with Parson Davis.

thirteen

Katie pulled a clothespin from her apron and hung another diaper on the line. The flannel squares snapped in the stiff breeze and would be dry in an hour. She picked up her empty basket and stared down the street.

Though she'd been at Alice Howard's home for a week, she still couldn't get used to living in town. Every direction she turned, there were houses or tall buildings blocking the view. Katie longed to jump on a horse and ride out to the open prairie, where the land rolled on until it reached the horizon.

She swiped at a tear tickling her cheek. Even worse was this horrible ache deep within her. She had never considered how much she would miss Dusty. Though soft-spoken, he was all man. Tall, strong, and even kind when she wasn't.

When she first returned to her aunt and uncle's after the fire, Dusty's visits irritated her, but at some point, she had begun to look forward to them. Now she longed to see his face again.

Was he angry with her for leaving without talking to him? Without telling him why she couldn't marry him?

She wondered for the thousandth time if she'd done the right thing in letting her uncle tell him. Katie closed her eyes. It cut her to the soul to think that she'd hurt such a good man.

And why did obeying God have to hurt so badly? If this was the right thing to do, shouldn't God take her pain away?

With a sigh, she hoisted the empty basket onto her hip and headed back to Alice Howard's white clapboard house.

The woman maintained a meticulous home. Though her old teacher seemed delighted to have Katie staying with her, Katie wondered how she would react once Joey started getting around and could bother her things.

With Alice gone all day teaching school, Katie had the house to herself. And way too much time to think.

In her heart, she knew she couldn't marry Dusty when he wasn't right with God. But why did it have to hurt so much?

The door clicked shut, and she set the basket in the kitchen. She needed to check on Joey, and then she'd go dump the rinse water on Alice's garden, though the only thing still growing were pumpkins.

She remembered how the twins had thought she had swallowed a pumpkin when she was carrying Joey. A wave of homesickness washed over her.

She moved slowly through the house, allowing her eyes to adjust to the dim light inside. Upstairs, she crossed the hall to her bedroom and peeked at her son. The blanket on his back rose and fell with his soft breathing. His tiny thumb lay just outside his open mouth.

Love for Joey surged through her. How was it possible to care so deeply for someone who'd been part of your life for such a short time?

She'd asked herself the same thing about Dusty—many times.

Her love for Jarrod had grown slower. She'd see him weekly at church services in Guthrie and occasionally at a barn raising or town event.

She'd never loved Allan. For some reason, she still had trouble thinking of him as Ed Sloane. Maybe doing so forced her to admit how wrong she'd been about the man. Why hadn't she yielded to the apprehension and doubt she had felt about marrying him?

It was pure stubbornness. She wanted to keep her land and was willing to do almost anything—and she nearly had.

Katie lay down on her bed, suddenly weary. Joey hadn't slept well since the move and was restless during the daytime. She suspected he missed all the attention he had gotten from her family.

Stuffing the pillow under her head, she longed for Aunt Rebekah's warm embrace. To see Deborah's quick smile or the twins whooping it up. She had wanted her independence, and now she had it. But she missed her family and Dusty something awful.

Tears stung her eyes and clogged her throat. Why did life have to be so difficult?

Her thoughts drifted back to Dusty. Was he still in Guthrie? Or had her desertion caused him to ride off in search of other outlaws?

She thought of the three letters she'd tried to pen him. None of her words seemed appropriate, and none relieved her guilt. She'd told him she loved him and would marry him but had ridden away without even a good-bye. Difficult as it would be, the next time she saw him, she'd need to apologize for running away without telling him why she was leaving.

A picture of Allan dressed in his swanky suit flittered across her mind. Then that miserable scene was obliterated with her first view of Dusty standing like a majestic warrior in her parlor with the wind whipping his long duster around his legs. His raven black eyes focused steadily on his prey. Who would have thought such a man capable of being so gentle and loving?

Overcome with homesickness and longing for Dusty, Katie turned her face into her pillow and wept. As she prayed, peace filled her soul. As hard as it was, she knew leaving her family and Dusty had been the right thing.

Every day as she prayed and drew closer to God, the aching lessened. Her problems were generated from her impulsiveness in plunging forward without seeking God's will first.

"Lord, forgive me for being so headstrong and independent. I need You. I need You to show me the way and to save me from myself and my hasty decisions. I promise to pray over decisions in the future and to never again charge forward like I know the answer to everything.

"And please, Father, if this gripping love I have for Dusty isn't from You—please take it away."

⁂

Dusty sang the words to "Amazing Grace" feeling as if the song had been written personally for him. He was the wretch that God had saved—the one who was lost, but now found.

And it felt so good to be back home with God.

Two weeks had passed since Katie had left, and he knew without a doubt that he loved her and wanted to marry her. But she had to be sure of that, too, and he was determined to give her all the time she needed to figure things out.

In the meantime, he'd strengthen his faith and become the man of God she needed.

He bowed his head for the closing prayer, then slowly made his way outside. After shaking the pastor's hand, he replaced his hat and nodded a greeting to several clusters of people as he passed them. His stomach growled, reminding him it was time for dinner. A warm meal at the café was just what he needed, and then he'd head over to his little rented house and finish painting the parlor.

If Katie ever decided she'd marry him, he wanted to have a place she'd feel comfortable calling home. If she never wanted to marry, he could always move out of the house. But he didn't like that alternative and prayed that God would speak to Katie and that her love for him was strong enough to endure this time of separation.

"Dusty!"

He looked up to see Mason jogging in his direction. Excitement zinged through him. He hadn't had a chance to tell Mason about his talk with Pastor Davis. Smiling, he held out his hand.

"Good to see you." Mason shook his hand. "I've been praying for you and wondering how you're doing. I was also hoping my talk with you wouldn't affect our friendship."

"Oh, it affected our friendship all right." Dusty struggled to keep a straight face.

Mason's eyebrows furrowed, and his lips tightened. "I'm real sorry to hear that."

"Don't be. I'm grateful you were a good enough friend to be honest with me. You made me realize that it was time I made things right with God. I had a long talk with the parson."

Mason's face beamed with joy. "You don't know how glad I am to hear that." He pulled Dusty into a bear hug and pounded on his shoulders. "That's the best news I've heard in weeks."

When Mason released him, Dusty stepped back and glanced around. He wasn't used to a man hugging him—or anyone, for that matter. He'd been a loner much too long.

"Now I understand."

"Understand what?" Dusty looked at Mason.

"God has been prompting me to ask you over for Thanksgiving dinner, but Rebekah thought I must have gotten into some locoweed." He grinned and peeked over his shoulder at his wife, who stood nearby talking with several women.

"Are you sure? I don't want to cause any trouble."

Mason nodded. "I'm sure. I've prayed about it for days. It wouldn't be a concern normally—you know you're welcome anytime—except that Katie is coming home for a week."

Dusty sucked in a gasp, then smiled. Would she notice a difference in him? Would she even want to see him? His joy deflated like a balloon. "I don't know if that's a good idea. Maybe she'll feel awkward with me there."

"I thought about that, too." Mason rubbed the back of his neck. "But I've prayed and believe this is what God wants. So you'll come?"

Dusty stared across the churchyard for a moment. How could he say no to seeing Katie and Joey again? "Yes, I'll come. Thank you for inviting me."

"There's just one thing. I hope you won't press Katie to marry you—now that you've made things right with God." Mason stared into Dusty's eyes, as if measuring his sincerity.

"I think you know I won't. I'm willing to wait until she knows her heart. It's like you said: If God wants us to be together, He'll work it out, and spending this time apart won't hurt things."

Mason nodded again and clasped Dusty's shoulders. "You make me proud to call you a friend. God always works things out. We'll see you on Thursday around noon."

Dusty watched Mason gather his family. He helped Rebekah onto the wagon seat and then lifted Deborah up beside her. Josh waved at him as he mounted his horse, and

Dusty waved back. The twins darted toward him, but a sharp yell from their father made them stop and return to the wagon.

Dusty didn't realize how much he'd missed Katie's family until he saw them again. He'd never been part of a large family, but he'd come to love the Danfields.

Jimmy walked toward him, leading his horse. "You've been a stranger lately."

Dusty shrugged, not sure what to say.

"I just wanted to tell you not to give up on Katie. We've talked, and I know her feelings for you run deep. She just needs some time to sort things out."

"Thanks. I'm trying to be patient, but I miss her more than I could have imagined. And little Joey, too."

"Katie's always been one to rush into things without thinking, but when she does step back and look at the whole picture, most of the time she'll make the right decision—as long as her stubbornness doesn't get in the way."

Jimmy offered a smile resembling Katie's so much that Dusty's insides clenched. He sorely missed her and could only pray she felt the same.

"Thanks for the encouragement. Will you be home for Thanksgiving? Mason invited me to dinner."

Jimmy gazed off into the distance. He had a restlessness about him that Dusty recognized because he'd once felt the same. A bolt of shock zigzagged through him as he realized he no longer had the restless spirit that made him travel from town to town, searching for outlaws for so long. He was ready to settle down again.

"I reckon I'll be there. But I've been thinking about going up to Tulsa. There's been several oil strikes there, and I've heard tell drilling companies are hurting for workers."

"Your family will miss you if you go."

Jimmy nodded. "And I'll miss them, but I can't explain this tugging I feel. It's almost as if I'm compelled to go."

Dusty wondered if it might somehow be God encouraging Jimmy to go, but he didn't see how any good could come of it. Katie had told him how restless Jimmy had been since he fought in the war.

"Have you tried praying about it?"

Jimmy scowled. "I don't pray anymore. It didn't do any good during the war, so I washed my hands of God."

Dusty laid his hand on Jimmy's shoulder. "I felt the same way, but Mason helped me see that I was wrong. God didn't move away from me; I moved away from Him."

Jimmy shrugged off Dusty's hand. "Yeah, well, that's fine for you, but I don't feel the same."

Dusty's heart ached for Jimmy as he watched him ride away. He looked around and realized they were the last two people left in the churchyard. As Dusty made his way toward the diner, he prayed for Jimmy. He knew so much of what Jimmy was feeling, but God had turned Dusty's life around; He could do the same for Katie's brother, too.

fourteen

Katie pulled the blue flannel gown over Joey's head and stuck his arms in the sleeves. Her little boy smiled up at her, turning her insides to warm grits. She'd never known such love in her life.

A soft knock sounded on her bedroom door, and Uncle Mason leaned against the door frame. "We all missed you while you were gone but understand your need to be independent."

"Thanks. It's so good to be home again, even if it's only for a visit." Katie smiled at her uncle as she slid the gown over Joey's wiggly legs. "I'm done here and should get downstairs and help with dinner."

"There's something I need to tell you." Her uncle rubbed the back of his neck, and apprehension washed over her at the familiar gesture. "Dusty's downstairs."

"What?" Katie pressed her hand to her chest, startled to the core.

"I invited him."

She sat on the edge of the bed as frustration battled excitement. "Why would you do that after you told me we couldn't marry?"

He straightened and shoved his hands in his pockets. "I never said you couldn't marry—just recommended against it at the time."

"But I still don't understand why you would invite him for

dinner, knowing I'd be here."

He pressed his lips together. "I can't say I understand, either, but I felt the Lord wanted me to invite him. Besides, it won't hurt you and him to talk. You did leave without saying good-bye."

Katie studied the dark red-and-blue-floral pattern on the rug. She knew leaving without talking to Dusty had been wrong. She needed to face him and apologize, and it looked like that would happen in the next few minutes.

Uncle Mason walked over to the bed. "Let me haul this critter downstairs for you."

"Why didn't you tell me sooner, so I had time to prepare?" Katie darted a glance in the oval mirror on the dresser, reattached some loose strands to the bun at her nape, and pinched her cheeks.

"You just would have worried and stewed over things like you are now." Joey squirmed and wiggled his arms as Mason tickled the boy's belly. He picked up her son and walked out into the hall, then turned around. "Don't be afraid to talk to Dusty. You might discover things have changed."

Katie wrinkled her brow. What could have changed in such a short time? Her love for him certainly hadn't. If anything, it had grown stronger, even though she'd begged God to take it away. With each step she took downstairs, her anxiety rose. Had the separation proven to Dusty that his feelings for her were false? Was that what Uncle Mason had meant?

The parlor was empty, so she followed her uncle into the kitchen where the family was already seated for dinner. The kitchen buzzed with excitement as the twins hovered around Jimmy and Josh, both talking at the same time. Deborah and Rebekah placed platters of fried chicken and biscuits onto the table. Dusty jumped to his feet and captured her gaze.

Katie's heart nearly stopped. For a time, it seemed as if no one else existed. Her heart pounded a ferocious tempo, and she wiped her slick palms on her skirt. Dusty's ebony eyes bore into hers, but she failed to interpret their message.

"Look who's here." Nate pounded Dusty on the shoulder, then sat next to him. "We ain't seen ol' Dusty in a coon's age."

"Stop hitting him, Nathan, and don't say ain't." Rebekah waved a spoon at her son.

The connection broken, Katie grabbed a bowl of mashed potatoes and set it on the table, then returned to the stove for green beans and sweet potatoes. When all the food was on the table, she took her seat across from Dusty. She needn't have pinched her cheeks because she was certain they were flaming after blatantly staring at Dusty like she'd done. It was so good to see him again.

Still, she couldn't help glancing up at him as she ate. There was something different about him, but she couldn't pinpoint it. He seemed to have a glow that wasn't there before.

The twins kept chattering, and Mason, Josh, and Jimmy talked about winter coming. Mason struggled to butter his biscuit as he held Joey in one arm. Katie pushed her plate back, having eaten only half her food. She was amazed she ate anything at all with Dusty constantly looking at her. "Pass Joey to me. I'm done."

Mason did as she requested, then picked up his fork in one hand and the knife in the other and dove into eating. Katie couldn't help smiling.

After enjoying her aunt's delicious sweet potato pie, she helped clean up the kitchen while Dusty and the men watched Joey. Katie dried a dish as she peered out the window. She longed to get out of the house to cool off from the hot kitchen and have time to think.

"I suppose you were surprised to see Dusty here." Her aunt glanced out the corner of her eye at her as she washed a mug.

"I can't deny it was quite a shock."

"He likes you." Deborah's youthful smile beamed from ear to ear.

Katie couldn't help giving her cousin a nudge with her hip. "You think so?"

Deborah nodded her head, making her opinion obvious.

"I tried to dissuade Mason from inviting him, thinking it would make things awkward for you." Rebekah set a cup in the rinse pan and gave her a sympathetic smile.

"It's all right. Honestly, I'm glad to see him again, even if we're only friends."

Rebekah's brows lifted, and she gave Katie a who-are-you-kidding smirk.

Katie heard Joey's frantic wail and could tell whoever was holding her son was coming toward her. Her heart nearly stopped when Dusty walked in, jiggling Joey on his shoulder.

"Sorry, but he only wants his mama."

Katie laid down the towel, walked into the hallway, and took the baby from Dusty, trying not to touch the man she loved for fear he'd sense her affection. Joey suddenly quieted and turned his face toward her chest, mouth open. Katie moved him to her shoulder, sure her cheeks were flaming. She followed Dusty down the short hall and stopped near the stairs.

"You want me to carry him up for you? Must be hard to manage stairs, a baby, and that long skirt."

Katie was moved by his concern. She jiggled Joey to keep

him from squawking. "I can manage, but thank you." She made the mistake of looking into his black eyes and lost herself there.

"I missed you, Katie." Dusty's lips tightened.

She looked away, then glanced back, knowing he deserved the truth. "I missed you, too, and I'm sorry for leaving without saying good-bye or explaining why I was going."

"It's all right. I understand your need to live somewhere other than here."

His compassion was almost her undoing, and tears blurred her vision.

Joey's patience evaporated, and the boy started crying. Katie jiggled him faster, but he wouldn't be soothed. "I need to feed him."

"Go ahead. We can talk later." Dusty lifted his hand and held it to her cheek. The look in his eyes took her breath away.

Half an hour later, Katie stood at the bedroom window, buttoning her blouse. As she tucked it into her wool skirt, she saw Dusty enter the barn with her uncle. Joey was asleep, and Dusty occupied, so now was her chance to take a walk.

She donned her cloak, thankful that Deborah had agreed to keep an eye on Joey. He'd eaten so well that he should sleep a good two hours or more, so she wasn't worried.

The chilly November breeze teased her cheeks and lifted loose strands of hair. Autumn was a pretty time of year, but she dreaded the upcoming winter. Even though winters were often mild in the Oklahoma Territory, the colder weather made life on a farm more difficult.

Her thoughts turned to Dusty. He'd looked better to her than Aunt Rebekah's pie. Even though her love for him hadn't diminished, there was still nothing to be done about it. She wouldn't marry a man who didn't love God as she did. She had nearly made that mistake twice, and it wouldn't happen again.

The dried grass crunched beneath her feet as she trod across the field toward the dirt road. It felt freeing to be out of the town, where she could see gently rolling hills clear to the horizon. The past few weeks away from home had given her plenty of time to read her Bible and seek God. She didn't understand why God hadn't taken away her love for Dusty, but rather than pine for him, she prayed.

"Father God." Katie stared up at the clear blue sky as she walked. "I ask You to take away Dusty's anger and unforgiving spirit over what Ed Sloane did to him. Bring Dusty back into the fold, so he can know Your love and not have to live alone. He's such a good man; You know how much I love him, but I give that love to You. If we are meant to be together someday, You'll have to make it happen."

A warmth flowed through her. Giving her love for Dusty to God was the right thing to do. She bent down to pick some burrs from her skirt, but when she looked up, she realized she had walked farther than she thought. She turned around and headed back to the house, which was a good mile away.

Behind her, she heard the pounding of horses' hooves and turned to see if a neighbor was coming to visit. She lifted her hand over her eyes and scanned the riders. Her heart nearly plunged to her feet. She sucked in a gasp. *No, it can't be.*

Katie lifted her skirts, turned back toward the farm, and ran for all she was worth. *Father, help me!*

The horses quickly closed the space, and Katie found herself surrounded by a pack of unkempt men whose expressions reminded her of ravenous wolves. The horses snorted and stamped their hooves. Katie stopped to catch her breath while her mind raced for a way to escape.

"Well, well, who would have thought you'd make things so easy?"

Katie cringed at the grating voice she had never expected to hear again. Gathering her courage, she turned to face Ed Sloane.

Though trembling so hard she feared her legs would give way, she hiked up her chin. Showing her fear would only please her ex-fiancé. "How did you get out of jail?"

His mouth, topped with a pencil-thin mustache she had once thought pleasing, turned up in an ugly sneer. "I always get out of jail, darlin'."

Katie dashed toward an opening between Ed's horse and another. Ed charged his mount forward to close the gap. He nodded at two riders behind her. Katie suddenly felt herself being lifted in the air by two of Sloane's henchmen and tossed in front of him on the horse. He'd slid back so that she now sat in his saddle. His arm slinked around her waist, and he tugged her back against his chest.

His warm breath touched her ear as he chuckled. "Well, well, you've lost some weight since I last saw you. Not bad."

Katie pried at his tight grasp with her fingers. "You let me go. I have a baby who needs me." She jabbed him with her elbow and kicked, making the horse prance sideways.

His grasp loosened, but when Katie prepared to lunge off the horse, the cold metal of a pistol to her temple froze her in place.

"You're coming with me, and there's no point fighting."

Katie blinked back her tears. Her throat burned. "Please,

my baby is dependent on me. I can't leave him behind."

"Too bad. If you want that sniffling baby to stay alive, you'd better cooperate."

Katie's heart thundered at the thought of Joey in Ed Sloane's evil hands, and she struggled to breathe.

She settled in for the ride, knowing she couldn't fight Sloane. For now, Joey would be safe with her family. They'd care for him. And her life would be in God's hands.

But how could she live without her son—even for a day?

And how could she live without Dusty for the rest of her life?

⁂

Dusty knocked on the kitchen door, and Rebekah looked up from her worktable. "Has Katie come back downstairs? I'd like to talk to her."

Rebekah nodded and wiped her hands on a towel. "Yes, she went for a walk close to an hour ago. She headed down the road away from town."

"Thanks." Dusty closed the door, walked to the barn, and saddled Shadow. If Katie had walked a long ways, she'd probably be relieved to have a ride back.

Excitement churned in his belly. He'd talked in the barn with Mason, and Mason agreed that Dusty should tell Katie how he'd made things right with God. She'd be so happy to learn he'd put his anger behind him and was ready to get on with his life. Mason had even told Dusty if Katie still wanted to marry him, he would give them his blessing as long as Dusty gave her the time she needed to decide.

He followed her footprints down the dirt road for close to a mile. His heart clenched. Fresh hoofprints surrounded Katie's prints. Dusty lifted his hat and stared out over the desolate landscape. Far off, he saw what looked to be dust stirred up by riders.

He swallowed hard and dismounted to examine the hoof marks. His eyes landed on a familiar square-shaped hoofprints made by Sloane's horse. Chills charged up his spine. The ache in his heart became a fiery gnawing. Sloane had Katie.

His Katie. The woman he loved with all his heart.

Dusty pressed his palms against his temples and cried out. "God, how could You let this happen again?"

He grabbed Shadow's reins, leaped onto the saddle, and kicked his mount forward. Suddenly, he reined the horse to a stop. He had taken off his holster at dinner and couldn't chase after Sloane unarmed. Stopped in the middle of the road, he wrestled between following his beloved and returning to the farm. Good sense won out over desperation, and he turned around, racing for the Danfield home.

fifteen

Armed with his pistol and a borrowed rifle, Dusty kicked Shadow into a gallop down the road after Katie. Mason and Jimmy followed right behind him. He'd lost valuable time going back, but at least he wouldn't have to face Sloane and his gang alone and unarmed.

How could Sloane have escaped again? And how did he manage to find Katie? Dusty pondered the questions for the hundredth time.

At a fork in the road, he dismounted and examined the hoofprints. Fortunately, with today being Thanksgiving and most people at home enjoying the holiday with their family, there weren't any other fresh prints on the road.

He glanced at the sky as he remounted. In another hour, it would be dark. Fear for Katie melded with a desperate need to hold her in his arms and make sure she was all right.

A heaviness pressed against his chest, making it hard to breathe. Somehow this had to be his fault. If he hadn't talked in the barn with Mason for so long, maybe he would have caught up with Katie before Sloane had. Or maybe. . .

No! He shook his head, refusing to give in to the negative thoughts that would steal his peace and try to sever his newly restored relationship with God.

This wasn't his fault, but he sure could change the outcome.

He nudged Shadow to go faster, all the time checking the trail and scouring the countryside for some sign of Katie. The giant orange orb of the soon-setting sun cast long shadows from the few trees on the prairie. When the sun set, so would any hopes of tracking Sloane and Katie.

God, please, help us find Katie before anything bad happens. Protect her.

Just before twilight, they reined their horses to a stop at a crossroads to give the animals a breather and to allow Dusty to check the trail. Several sets of hoofprints covered the area. Finally he decided to take the path to the right. They walked their horses so Dusty could scour the trail for signs of Sloane's gang.

After a few minutes, Dusty halted and stooped, examining the ground.

"What's wrong?" Mason stopped his mount beside him.

Dusty pressed his lips together, hating to admit the truth. "We turned the wrong way. I haven't seen Sloane's trail once since we took this path.

"Then let's go back to the fork and go the other way." Jimmy didn't wait for confirmation but spurred his horse around and into a run.

Dusty and Mason joined him and were soon back at the fork in the road. Dusty clenched his teeth together, angry with himself for wasting valuable time going the wrong way.

He studied the path as they walked the horses. The tracks angled off the road and onto a faint trail through the tall grass. Up ahead, Dusty could make out the beginnings of a large wooded area. If Sloane wanted to hide, that would be the place.

Mason and Jimmy moved up beside him and examined the ground. "What do you think? Will they ride all night or make camp somewhere?"

Dusty shrugged, wishing he knew for certain. If Sloane did make camp and they continued their search in the dark, they could ride right past him and his cohorts without knowing it.

He stared at the woods. "Sloane's a creature of comfort. My gut instinct says he'll make camp, but I don't know for sure. He's smart, but sometimes he underestimates people."

"You think he'd leave a guard behind?" Jimmy glanced at the woods and back at Dusty, then pulled his rifle from the scabbard. "We could be riding into a trap."

"Could be. What do you want to do?" He studied both men, unwilling to put their lives on the line. Even if they backed down, he knew he'd continue his search. He wouldn't quit until he rescued Katie.

"We've got to find her." Mason pressed his lips tight.

"But you have a family depending on you. Maybe you should ride back and let Jimmy and me continue."

Mason shook his head. "I'm not going back without Katie. Let's quit burning daylight."

Dusty nodded, relieved Mason was still at his side. As he stuck his foot in the stirrup, he heard the faint sound of a man's laughter, far off in the woods. He settled in his saddle and looked at Mason. "Did you hear that?"

"Sure did. What do you make of it?"

He held his finger to his lips. "Listen."

All three men held their horses steady and turned an ear toward the trees. A faint breeze blew in Dusty's face as he listened intently. He caught a few words of a man's curse, and his skin crawled. He'd recognize Ed Sloane's voice any day.

"That's him. I heard Sloane."

They secured their mounts to a lone tree and slowly crept through the tall prairie grass toward the edge of the woods. A hundred feet inside the tree line, the voices grew loud enough that they could make out all the words. Dusty peered around the side of a thick oak tree.

"We ought to keep going. We're too close to her home to stop." One of Sloane's cronies stood with his hands on his hips.

Sloane rubbed a finger over his thin mustache. "It's getting dark, and they probably haven't even missed her yet. I think we're safe here."

Dusty scanned the area, looking for Katie's rose-colored dress. When two men stepped forward to join the discussion, he saw her sitting in front of a tree, her hands tied and her eyes wide. Anger at Sloane for causing her fright roared through him like a wildfire, but at the same time, he ached to march in and comfort Katie. He pressed his hat down, ready to do battle for the woman he loved.

He whispered to Mason and Jimmy to make their way around, one to the right and one to the left. If push came to shove, they just might be able to fool Sloane and his gang into thinking they were surrounded. Dusty was thankful that the family had taken time to hold hands and pray for Katie and their safe return before they had left the house.

Joey's fervent cries for his mother echoed in Dusty's mind. *I'll get your mother home to you, little buddy. Just hang on.*

"Tell you what, I'd like a little time alone with my bride. You men go ahead and make for the hideout. Me and the little woman will get reacquainted."

Even from this distance, Dusty saw the panic that crossed Katie's face. She didn't want to be left alone with Sloane. She closed her eyes, and Dusty hoped she was praying. They'd need all the prayers they could muster to capture Sloane again.

હ

Katie's heart pounded in her chest as she watched Sloane argue with his men. She hoped they'd stay here and make camp to give Dusty a chance to catch up, but she didn't want to be alone with Sloane. She knew Dusty would come looking for her and blessed God that her uncle had invited him for dinner. She hated to think of her sweet uncle and brother going up against Sloane without Dusty's experience and help.

Katie's shoulders ached from tension, and her whole body trembled. She longed to see Joey and wondered again what Rebekah would do when he got hungry. Maybe she'd make him some warm sugar water, but would that satisfy her famished son?

Father God, please watch over Joey and help him. Show Dusty the way to find me. And soon, Lord. Please. I don't want to be alone with this evil man.

Tears stung her eyes. How could she ever have considered marrying Sloane? How could she have been so desperate that she had been swayed by his counterfeit charm?

She no longer thought him appealing, only despicable. And evil.

She longed for a bath to wash his touch off her skin.

Her stomach churned at the thought of riding with him again. His whispered words of romance and what he had planned for her chilled her to the core. Shivering, she watched with dread as Sloane's men mounted their horses and rode off. Soon the last faint rays of the sun, which painted the dusky sky bright pink and orange, would fade, and she'd be left alone in the dark with this dark man.

God, no. Please, Lord.

One horseman reined in his mount and turned around.

Katie held her breath. "Are you certain you want us all to leave? What if they catch up with you?"

"They won't catch me in the dark. I don't need a fire for what I have planned, and I don't need an audience."

"All right then. See you at camp, boss."

The man rode off, taking with him Katie's last hope of not being alone with Sloane. She quivered, knowing exactly how a rabbit felt caught in a snare. She searched for some way of escape and wrestled with the rope that held her hands captive until it bit into her skin. The glint in Sloane's eyes as he talked about his plans for her threatened to cut her fragile thread of control.

A chilling silence surrounded them and grew tight with tension. Sloane stared at the woods as if searching for someone, then finally faced her. A knot formed in her stomach as his gaze traveled over her.

Father, give me strength.

"You don't know how long I've dreamed of this moment while I spent those weeks in that rotten jail." He leaned forward, his eyes narrowed. "Thoughts of having my way with you kept me going," he said in a frigid whisper.

Sick to her stomach, Katie swallowed. *Help me, Lord. Help me.*

Though frightened beyond anything she'd ever experienced, Katie felt God's peace surround her like a woolen cloak. Somehow, she'd make it through this night.

Sloane stood and shed his jacket. "You know, I never really wanted to marry you. I just needed your land—to fund my gambling operation up in Kansas. But by marrying you, I got you and your land—or would have if that stupid marshal turned bounty hunter hadn't interfered. He's next on my list—after I take care of you."

Katie shuddered. She didn't want to die but knew in her heart that her family would take care of Joey and raise him up properly. At the thought of never seeing Joey, Dusty, or her family again, tears coursed down her cheeks.

Her aunt had been right in saying that Dusty had saved her from marrying an outlaw. She shivered as Sloane unbuttoned his vest and dropped it on the ground. If only Dusty could save her again.

sixteen

Sloane yanked his shirttail from his trousers and began unbuttoning his shirt. Frantic, Katie tore with her teeth at the rope that held her bound. Maybe, just maybe, if she could get loose, she could put up a good fight. She was no longer the slow, cumbersome woman that he had known when she was with child.

Maybe she could stall and give Dusty more time to find her. "Why me? I mean, there are widows all over the Oklahoma Territory. Why did you choose me?"

Sloane's arrogant chuckle resonated in the air and sent goose bumps charging up her arms. The cool breeze blew dust against her cheeks and made her shiver.

"I was in the right place at the right time. Saw you crossing the street in Claremont. You pulled off your hat and made an adjustment to it, and the sun glistened on that yellow hair of yours. At the same time, two women passed by me and muttered something about how it was a shame that you were a widow at such a young age." He rubbed his finger over his thin mustache. "Didn't take long to find out where you lived and learn your farm was for sale."

Sloane turned his back to her, sauntered over to his horse, and took a slow drink from his canteen.

Katie struggled to her feet. If she couldn't get her hands free, at least she could run. She looked to her left and then right as she tried to figure out the best direction to go. If she got far enough away, Sloane might not be able to find her once the sun set. She lunged to her right, away from her captor, but she stepped on the hem of her skirt and nearly fell. She glanced over her shoulder. Panic bolted through her.

Leaves crunched under his feet as Sloane stomped toward her, evil glimmering in his icy blue eyes. He grabbed her by the shoulders, spun her around, and pulled her toward him. She shoved against his chest and felt a small victory when he winced from the abrasive rope scratching his skin.

He held her against him, Katie's left arm crushed against the cold metal of a pistol in his waistband. If only she could get ahold of it, then maybe she'd have a chance.

Sloane grabbed her hair, which had long since come loose of its pins, and he yanked her head back. Katie grimaced from the pain.

"I like a woman who doesn't give in easily."

Katie quivered as his lips angled toward hers. Suddenly, she heard a click, and Sloane froze, his eyes wide open.

"Let that woman go—or you're a dead man."

Katie gasped at the sound of Dusty's voice, low and calculated. She saw the indecision in Sloane's eyes. Then he shoved her away so fast that she fell to the ground, landing on her backside.

Katie's heart leaped at the sight of the man she loved standing there with his hat pulled low, pistol aimed at Sloane, and his duster flapping in the breeze, looking like a warrior.

"Get those hands up where I can see them."

Sloane lifted his left hand, but ever so slowly, his right hand eased toward the weapon in his waistband.

"Look out! He's got a gun!" Katie screamed.

Dusty glanced at her, and in that split second, Sloane

grabbed his pistol and pointed it at her. Katie squeezed her eyes shut, certain she'd never see her baby again.

The nearby blast of a gun echoed in her ear, making her jump. She winced, waiting—expecting—to feel pain, but when she didn't, she opened her eyes, taking in the scene before her.

Sloane lay on the ground, grasping his arm and cursing in pain. Mason and Jimmy stood beside him with their rifles pointed at him. Dusty stepped through a cloud of gun smoke and hurried to her side. He scooped her up in his arms and held her tight.

Tears of joy and relief streamed down Katie's cheeks.

"I thought I'd lost you," Dusty whispered in her ear.

He held her so tight Katie could barely breathe. "If you could untie me, I could hug you back properly."

Dusty blinked in confusion, then looked at her hands. "Oh, sorry." He gently set her down and pulled a knife from his boot. Ever so carefully, he slit the rope, freeing her hands. Katie rolled her shoulders, then rubbed her wrists while Dusty put away his knife.

"You're bleeding." He took her wrists and examined them, placing tiny kisses close to the scrapes.

Katie stepped into his arms, feeling safer than she ever had. This man she loved would protect her, even at the cost of his own life.

❧

Jimmy started a fire while Uncle Mason tied up Sloane and tended to his wounds. Katie winced as Dusty dabbed a damp handkerchief on the scratches on her wrists. He hated that she'd been hurt but was so grateful to God that they found her before something worse had happened.

He kissed her wrists again; then they walked away from Sloane's menacing gaze. Dusty kept a firm hold on Katie's arm so that she didn't stumble. When they were in the shadows but could still see the light of the campfire, he stopped and turned her to face him.

"I knew you'd come." Katie's breath was warm against his cheeks. "I prayed you would find me."

Dusty ran his hand over her head and down to her soft cheek. "I couldn't stand the thought that Sloane had you. I'd have searched the whole nation to find you."

Dusty gently pulled Katie against his chest and laid his cheek on her hair. "I love you, Katie."

She leaned back and looked up at him. He could barely make out the right side of her face, illuminated by the campfire. She gazed at him for a long while. "I love you, too, Dusty. I've tried not to, but I can't help it. But that doesn't mean there's a future for us. I can't marry a man who doesn't love God and doesn't put the Lord first in his life."

Despite her words, hope soared in his chest, and love for this woman made his knees weak. He cupped her cheek in his hand. "Then I guess it's a good thing I made peace with God, isn't it?"

Katie gasped. "What? You did?"

Dusty nodded. "Yes. I had a long talk with Mason. I realized that he and I were in the same boat: Both of us lost our wives due to tragic circumstances. Mason had been angry with God for a time, just like I was. I didn't think God would forgive me for walking away from Him when things got tough. But Mason had done the same thing, and if God could forgive him, He could forgive me."

Katie fell into his arms. "Oh, Dusty, you don't know how

happy that makes me. I longed for you to make peace with God and to lose your anger over Emily's death."

Dusty chuckled. "I guess I owe Sloane a big thank-you."

Katie leaned back but didn't step out of his arms. "Why ever for?"

"If I hadn't found Sloane at your house like I did, I'd probably never have met you."

"Oh!"

He placed his hands on Katie's cheeks. "I'm going to kiss you now—unless you don't want me to."

Proving she had no objections, she leaned forward. His lips touched her velvet-soft lips, and Dusty's pulse leaped as if he'd been plugged into one of those new electric lights. Katie's arms went around his neck and pulled him closer. She kissed him back with a promise of their future together. Too soon, he pulled back, his breath ragged.

Katie touched his cheek. "I love you so much, Dusty."

He wanted to stand there and kiss her all night but was afraid her brother and uncle might shoot him like one of them had Sloane. "I love you, too, Katie. Is it too soon to ask you to marry me again?"

She shook her head no and opened her mouth to respond, but he placed his finger over her lips.

"Before you answer, there's a condition."

Katie's eyebrows dipped. "What condition?"

"That you don't run away this time."

Her lips parted in a wide grin. "I can assure you, that won't happen. In fact, you'll have a difficult time getting away from me. I would love nothing more than to marry you."

He kissed her again and then reluctantly escorted her back to the camp. Mason and Jimmy strode forward and enveloped Katie in a hug. Mason glanced over her head and looked at Dusty with a questioning gaze. Dusty couldn't hold back his grin, and he nodded his head to let Mason know Katie had agreed to marry him.

seventeen

Dusty's heart pounded as he rode into Sanders Creek. The last time he'd been in his hometown was the day his life had changed forever. But he knew in order to move on and begin a new life with Katie, he had to close the door on his past life—and the only way to do that was to return to Sanders Creek.

The town had changed in the time he'd been gone. New buildings had sprung up, and older ones had been repainted or spruced up. People ambled along the boardwalk, while a few wagons and riders on horseback dotted the dirt street. He could hear the sounds of an active town—a blacksmith hammering, a train whistling, and some cattle lowing. Fragrant aromas from the café wafted on the morning breeze. Life had continued here as if nothing bad had ever happened.

His gaze was automatically drawn toward the marshal's office. A man sat polishing a rifle in a chair that hadn't been outside the office when he was marshal. The man watched him with interest. He slowed his polishing, then leaned the rifle against the clapboard wall and stood. He sauntered over and rested his shoulder against a pole holding up the overhanging roof.

Dusty's heart pinged as he recognized his old friend Tom. The man now wore the marshal's badge on his vest. A slow smile brightened Tom's craggy features. " 'Bout time you returned. Folks pretty much gave up on ever seeing you again, but I told them you'd be back. Course, if you're planning on gettin' your old job back as marshal, you've got a fight on your hands."

Dusty slid off Shadow, hopped up the steps, and shook Tom's hand. "Your job is safe. I've got my own job back in Guthrie."

"Guthrie! Whatcha doing there?"

"It's a long story, trust me."

Tom leaned back and crossed his arms over his chest. "Did you ever catch that fellow who—well, you know."

Dusty nodded, glad to have good news to share. "Ed Sloane is finally in the state penitentiary, along with the rest of his gang. There's no longer anyone running loose who can rescue him." He'd spent two weeks chasing the men who had helped kidnap Katie, making sure that he caught every last one of them. He never wanted to have another encounter with Ed Sloane again.

He studied his friend. Tom had barely aged since he'd last seen him, making Dusty wonder if he himself had. Life on the trail hadn't been easy and must have taken a toll on him. "How's the shoulder?"

Tom flexed his arm. "Good as new, though it was slow going at first. Came as close to meeting my Maker back then as I ever have. Took a good two months before I could work again."

"Glad to hear it's better. I'm sorry you got caught in all that mess."

Tom shrugged. "It's just part of the job."

Dusty looked down the street, not really wanting to voice his next question but knowing he must. "Whatever happened to my old house?"

Tom narrowed his eyes. "Guess you knew about the fire, huh?"

Dusty nodded.

"Well, Lawrence Spenser, the man who owned that property, had the mess cleaned up and a new house built there. Then he sold it to a family new to town."

Dusty clenched his jaw. "And what about Emily?"

Tom's lips tightened, and he looked away. "Her pa had her buried in the town graveyard right after the fire. They waited a month for you to return before finally going ahead with the funeral."

"Guess I'd better head over there and say my good-byes."

Tom studied him. "So you don't plan on staying around these parts?"

"No." Dusty shook his head. "I'm a deputy marshal in Guthrie. Figure I'll stay on there." Finally he smiled. "Met a feisty little gal that I'm getting ready to marry."

Tom's cheeks pulled up in a grin. "I'm right glad to hear that. You deserve to find some happiness after all you've been through."

Dusty shook his friend's hand and rode over to the grave-yard. Birds chattered and chirped their cheerful songs, which seemed out of place for a cemetery. He tied Shadow to the picket fence. The three-foot-high gate screeched as he entered.

He wandered around, passing mostly the graves of people whose names he didn't recognize. He nearly stumbled when his gaze landed on the recent grave of Jed Harper, the old man who'd been his neighbor. Beside Mr. Harper, Dusty noticed the grave of Mrs. Harper. She had died only a few days after the fire that killed Emily. He wondered if those traumatic events had been too much for the sickly woman.

He meandered toward the back of the graveyard, his eyes scanning for Emily's grave. His gaze landed on a grave with an iron fence surrounding it, and he felt pulled in that direction. Emily's wealthy parents would have wanted something that nice for her.

His heart jolted when his gaze collided with the white marble tombstone. EMILY ANDERSON MCINTYRE. BELOVED WIFE AND DAUGHTER. 1883–1903. HERE ONLY A BRIEF TIME, BUT SHE TOUCHED MANY LIVES.

Dusty wished it was the season for flowers so he could lay some on the grave, but instead he twisted his hat in his hands. Emily's parents had picked a nice spot for her grave. Several dogwood trees and a redbud stood behind the headstone. In the spring, they would add the pretty colors Emily had cherished. A shallow creek trickled along about fifty feet from the edge of the cemetery.

Dusty stared at the tombstone. "I miss you, Em. I want you to know I caught that scoundrel who was responsible for our troubles, and he'll never hurt another innocent soul again. I'm so sorry for the pain he caused you and for not being able to rescue you."

Dusty wiped his damp eyes on his sleeve. "I want you to know I'm getting married again. You'd like Katie. She's pretty and spunky and has the cutest little boy who needs a pa.

"I can't pretend to understand why God took you home to be with Him. All I can think of is Katie needed me more. And I need her. You'll be happy to know I've made peace with God."

Dusty pressed his lips together. Sanders Creek had been his home the first part of his life, but his future rested in Guthrie. With his good-byes said, he smacked on his hat and mounted

Shadow. Excitement coursed through him as he thought of his future.

"Let's go, boy. Katie's awaiting."

&

Katie studied the reflection of her new dress in Rebekah's tall oval mirror. The ecru-colored fabric fitted her narrow waist and lay in soft pleats around her hips. Irish lace at the neck and cuffs gave it a bit of fluff, but it was still sensible enough that it could serve as her Sunday dress after the wedding.

A delicious shiver of excitement wound its way through her, making her stomach queasy. She shoved another pin in her hair and patted one side, hoping her curls would stay put throughout the day's activities.

Rebekah strolled in, holding Joey against her shoulder. "You look beautiful, dear."

Katie smiled. She felt beautiful and hoped that Dusty would agree.

"So, no regrets?"

"No, not a one. Well, except I'm still not sure about leaving Joey here with you all overnight. He hasn't yet taken a bottle."

Her aunt patted Joey's padded bottom. "He will when he gets hungry enough."

"I just hate leaving him—after what happened."

Rebekah wrapped her arm around Katie's shoulders. "I know, but that's in the past. We'll take good care of him for you."

Katie moved behind Rebekah and looked at her son's face. His eyes were shut, and his thumb rested in his mouth. How could she bear to leave him overnight?

"I know what you're thinking, but he'll be just fine. He knows us and can get by without you for such a short time. Besides, you and Dusty need time alone on your wedding night."

Katie touched her warm cheeks, making her aunt grin. She had no concerns or fears about her wedding night with Dusty. She was certain that if she loved him any more, she just might explode. No, she had no regrets. Not a one.

Deborah glided into the room in her new, rose-colored dress. "Oh, you look so pretty!"

Katie took hold of both her hands and studied her cousin, then gave the girl a hug. "So do you."

Deborah's cheeks turned bright red. "Thank you. Pa says it's time to go."

With hands shaking from excitement, Katie donned her cloak and headed for the wagon that would take them to the Christmas Eve service, followed by her wedding. The month she and Dusty had waited after agreeing to marry had been the longest of her life. But this time, she hadn't rushed into things. She had taken the time to pray and make sure that marrying Dusty was God's will for her life. It amazed her how she'd come full circle and was once again starting her life over. She'd sold her land and had put the money in a savings account. They used some of the funds to buy a house in Guthrie so she could stay near her family and Dusty could keep his job, and what was left over would be saved so that Joey could attend college one day or buy his own land.

Uncle Mason's eyes beamed as he lifted her into the fancy buggy he'd borrowed just for the day. Today she and Dusty would marry, and tomorrow they'd celebrate their first Christmas together with the family.

❧

Dusty straightened his new suit for the hundredth time and tugged at the string tie at his neck. Only for Katie would he wear the crazy thing that nearly choked off his breath. He figured he knew what a calf felt like when some cowpoke lassoed it.

"Stand still. You're gonna have folks thinking you're about ready to bolt." Jimmy chuckled in Dusty's ear. Serving as best man, he looked just as uncomfortable as Dusty felt. "It's not too late to salvage your freedom before you're tied to my sister's apron strings for life."

He didn't think he'd mind that one bit, but this waiting up in front of the whole community was getting old. "I thought the women were ready to get this show on the road."

Jimmy shrugged, and the pastor cleared his throat and gave them a stern look.

The pastor's wife began an elegant tune on the pump organ. The whole church was filled with their friends and townsfolk. Josh stood in the back, serving as usher. Deborah, looking pretty and mature in her new pink dress, entered the back of the church. A combination maid of honor and flower girl, she dropped flower petals along the aisle floor and took her place as maid of honor next to where Katie would stand. A faint floral scent wafted in the air as she passed by. Dusty couldn't imagine where the women had found flower petals in December.

The twins, dressed in white shirts and dark pants, began their walk down the aisle. Each boy held one side of a frilly pillow to which Katie's wedding ring was tied. All the men had questioned the females as to the sense of allowing the feisty boys such an important duty, but the women were certain the twins would behave.

Nathan tugged on the pillow. "You're holding too much," he whispered, loud enough that Dusty heard up front.

"Nuh-uh. You are." Nick gave a little yank and regained his hold.

Nathan scowled and pressed his lips together. Dusty watched Rebekah glare at the boys from her perch in the front row. Suddenly, Nathan jerked on the pillow. It went sailing into Homer Johnson's head and then bounced onto the aisle floor. Stunned shock widened Mr. Johnson's eyes; then his lips twitched, and he burst out laughing, many in the audience joining him.

Both boys lunged forward at the same time. Nick fell on top of the pillow, and Nathan fell on Nick.

"I got it! Get off me!" Nick screamed.

Rebekah leaped to her feet, handed Joey to Mrs. Whitaker in the second-row pew, and marched down the aisle. Men chuckled, and women stared wide-eyed at the wrestling boys. Dusty had a feeling this wedding would be talked about for weeks.

Rebekah grabbed both boys by the earlobes and tugged them to the front row. Once seated, the twins nudged each other with their elbows. Dusty couldn't help smiling.

Rebekah retrieved the pillow, handed it to Jimmy, and then sat down between her two sons.

"But we's s'posed to be up there with Jimmy and Dusty," Nick whined.

At his mother's stern glare, the boy crossed his arms and hunkered down, glowering.

"Bet you never forget that." Jimmy chuckled softly beside Dusty as he untied the ring and tossed the lacy pillow aside. "Good thing Katie didn't see it."

Dusty grinned. He heard a ruckus at the back and saw Mason and Katie enter the church. The music became louder, and the organist played another tune.

Dusty held his breath as Katie glided down the church aisle

toward him. Her pale-colored dress emphasized her tanned skin. He loved that she wasn't afraid to allow the sun to color her skin. It made her blue eyes stand out that much more. Her glorious, golden hair was piled on top of her head in delicate curls. He couldn't wait until he had the right to yank out all those pins and run his hands through her flaxen mane.

Mason walked with Katie on his arm. His eyes beamed with pride, making Dusty glad they'd waited to marry until both Mason and Rebekah could give their blessing.

Katie's eyes gleamed. His insides turned somersaults. Oh, how he loved this woman! Mason handed her off, and Dusty took his beloved's hand and turned to face the minister.

It amazed him how God had taken a man filled with anger and grief and washed him clean, even giving him a future as a husband and father. Only God's forgiving grace could change a man that much.

Dusty glanced at the cross behind the minister's head as he listened to Katie pledge her love.

Thank You, God, for new beginnings.

A Letter To Our Readers

Dear Reader:

In order that we might better contribute to your reading enjoyment, we would appreciate your taking a few minutes to respond to the following questions. We welcome your comments and read each form and letter we receive. When completed, please return to the following:

Fiction Editor
Heartsong Presents
PO Box 719
Uhrichsville, Ohio 44683

1. Did you enjoy reading *The Bounty Hunter and the Bride* by Vickie McDonough?
   ❑ Very much! I would like to see more books by this author!
   ❑ Moderately. I would have enjoyed it more if

   _____

   _____

   _____

2. Are you a member of **Heartsong Presents**? ❑ Yes ❑ No
   If no, where did you purchase this book? _____

   _____

3. How would you rate, on a scale from 1 (poor) to 5 (superior), the cover design? _____

4. On a scale from 1 (poor) to 10 (superior), please rate the following elements.

   ____ Heroine   ____ Plot
   ____ Hero   ____ Inspirational theme
   ____ Setting   ____ Secondary characters

5. These characters were special because? _____

_____

_____

6. How has this book inspired your life? _____

_____

_____

7. What settings would you like to see covered in future
   Heartsong Presents books? _____

_____

_____

8. What are some inspirational themes you would like to see
   treated in future books? _____

_____

_____

9. Would you be interested in reading other **Heartsong
   Presents** titles?   ❏ Yes   ❏ No

10. Please check your age range:
     ❏ Under 18   ❏ 18-24
     ❏ 25-34   ❏ 35-45
     ❏ 46-55   ❏ Over 55

Name _____

Occupation _____

Address _____

City, State, Zip _____

BROTHERS
OF THE OUTLAW TRAIL

4 stories in 1

Four first-rate authors bring the outlaw Wilson brothers—Reuben, Caleb, Colt, and Benjamin—to life in this daring collection of stories set in the historic Wild West. As the tales unfold, the reader is in for a feast of adventure, romance, and the transforming grace of faith in God.

Historical, paperback, 352 pages, 5³⁄₁₆" x 8"

———————————————————

Please send me ____ copies of *Brothers of the Outlaw Trail*.
I am enclosing $6.97 for each.
(Please add $2.00 to cover postage and handling per order. OH add 7% tax.)

Send check or money order, no cash or C.O.D.s, please.

Name_____

Address _____

City, State, Zip _____

To place a credit card order, call 1-740-922-7280.
Send to: Heartsong Presents Readers' Service, PO Box 721, Uhrichsville, OH 44683